Gabby smiled. "Would you like to pet her?

Noah was floored that Gabby would allow that, given how Sloane had acted this morning.

"Yeah!" Sloane said. She started toward the dog.

"Wait," Gabby said firmly, stepping in front of her. "There are conditions."

Sloane tipped her head to one side, obviously unsure of the meaning of the word.

"The conditions are that you can't pick her up or hold on to her if she wants to leave, and you can only pet her with two fingers, like we talked about before." She studied Sloane. "Go ahead, sit beside her and show me you understand."

After a moment's hesitation, Sloane nodded. "Okay!" She walked over to the dog, sat down beside her and petted her with two fingers.

Noah closed his eyes for a brief moment.

Maybe this could work. It was clear that Gabby was fantastic at managing kids, and that she didn't get thrown off or hold a grudge when one acted out.

She'd make a good mother for Sloane.

Lee Tobin McClain is the *New York Times* bestselling author of emotional small-town romances featuring flawed characters who find healing through friendship, faith and family. Lee grew up in Ohio and now lives in Western Pennsylvania, where she enjoys hiking with her goofy goldendoodle, visiting writer friends and admiring her daughter's mastery of the latest TikTok dances. Learn more about her books at leetobinmcclain.com.

Books by Lee Tobin McClain

Love Inspired

K-9 Companions

Her Easter Prayer
The Veteran's Holiday Home
A Friend to Trust
A Companion for Christmas
A Companion for His Son
His Christmas Salvation
The Veteran's Valentine Helper
Holding Onto Secrets
Her Surprise Neighbor

Rescue Haven

The Secret Christmas Child
Child on His Doorstep
Finding a Christmas Home

Visit the Author Profile page at LoveInspired.com for more titles.

HER SURPRISE NEIGHBOR

LEE TOBIN McCLAIN

Love Inspired
INSPIRATIONAL ROMANCE

LOVE INSPIRED®
INSPIRATIONAL ROMANCE

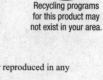

ISBN-13: 978-1-335-62109-2

Her Surprise Neighbor

Recycling programs
for this product may
not exist in your area.

Love Inspired
22 Adelaide St. West, 41st Floor
Toronto, Ontario M5H 4E3, Canada
www.LoveInspired.com

Printed in Lithuania

MIX
Paper | Supporting
responsible forestry
FSC® C021394

And we know that all things work together for good
to them that love God, to them who are the called
according to his purpose.
—*Romans* 8:28

To adoptive and birth families everywhere.

Chapter One

On a Wednesday night in August, a high-pitched scream awakened Gabby Dunn. Caramel, her Yorkie, raced to the foot of the bed, then back to Gabby, yipping.

Gabby sat straight up, her heart pounding, her adrenaline racing. Moonlight illuminated her small, neat bedroom. No shadows. No intruders.

She reached for Caramel and cuddled her close, stroking the dog and taking deep breaths.

She was safe. Safe in her little home in her aunt's cottage resort on the Chesapeake Bay. Seven years safe from the double trauma that had nearly ruined her life.

"Mama's silly," she said to Caramel, and the Yorkie licked her face.

Another scream broke the nighttime silence. It sounded like a child. A little girl. Was she dreaming?

A car door slammed. Caramel struggled in Gabby's arms, barking again.

Through her screened bedroom window, Gabby heard a man's voice. "Stop it right now."

Worry gripped Gabby's heart.

Was the child hurt? Was the man mistreating her?

Gabby threw on a hoodie, grabbed her phone and Caramel, and walked outside.

Caramel yipped again. "Quiet," Gabby ordered, and the dog obeyed.

The porch light revealed a late-model SUV, parked in front of the cottage next door. The child's cries came from the other side of the vehicle. Phone in hand, Gabby tiptoed around the vehicle.

A man knelt on the ground, his voice rumbling but calm as a child yelled and struck at him.

It *was* a little girl, probably seven or eight, wearing Super Kat pajamas. Her blond hair was shoulder-length, stringy and rumpled. She wore a rubber Crocs shoe on one foot. The other was bare.

"I want candy, Daddy! Right now!"

Gabby's shoulders relaxed, and she shoved her phone into the pocket of her flannel pajama pants. The man was the little girl's father, and he wasn't doing anything except trying to calm down his child.

"We can go see your new bedroom when you settle down," he said. It was amazing that his voice remained calm in the face of the child's escalating cries.

Gabby cleared her throat to let the pair know she was there, but neither man nor child noticed. She needed a better distraction. "Speak," she ordered Caramel.

The little dog barked, once. "Good girl," Gabby murmured. "Speak."

Caramel barked again, and this time, both father and daughter turned toward Gabby and Caramel.

"Hi," Gabby said. "I live next door." She nodded sideways toward her cottage. "Is there any way I can help?"

The little girl went silent. She stared at Caramel.

The man took the child's hand and they moved a couple of steps closer. A motion sensor light came on and she saw him more clearly.

Wow.

He wasn't exactly handsome. His face was a little too square and strong-boned for that. His hair was cut short, militarily so, and he wore a short-sleeved plaid shirt and faded jeans. His arms were brawny. His whole *self* was brawny.

It was Gabby's favorite look.

And how ridiculous that she was thinking such a thing at this hour, in this situation.

An angelic smile crossed the little girl's tear-streaked face. She lifted a hand toward Caramel. "Can I hold her?"

"No," the dad said quickly. He shook his head at Gabby.

She wouldn't have allowed it, anyway; Caramel was mighty of spirit but she was small. Children had to be taught to be gentle before Gabby would allow them full access to her dog. "Not tonight, honey," she said. "But you can talk to her while your dad carries in your things."

"I. Want. To. Hold. Her!" The child's voice got louder with each word. She pulled her hand from her father's, ran to Gabby and started jumping up at Caramel.

Gabby turned away to protect the dog.

"Sorry, sorry," the man said. He reached for the little girl and held her by her shoulders. "We need to be gentle and listen."

"It's okay," Gabby assured him. "I'm a teacher. I'm used to kids. Go ahead and unpack." She looked down at the little girl with a reassuring smile. "How old are you?" she asked. A sudden change of topic often worked with her second graders. Maybe it would work with this little girl.

"Seven," the child said, with a momentary pause in the jumping.

"And what's your name?"

"Sloane."

Gabby smiled, relieved that her strategy was working. "That's a pretty name."

The man mouthed, *Thank you*, and jogged to the back of his vehicle. He started pulling suitcases out.

"I wanna hold the dog." Sloane reached for Caramel again. This time, her hand swiped Caramel's tail.

"No. Not tonight." Again, Gabby turned so Sloane couldn't reach the dog.

Sloane's mouth opened in a round O. Her scream was piercing.

"Sloane!" The stranger dropped the suitcases he was carrying. He strode over and picked up his child.

Gabby frowned. She loved kids, and knew a lot about them after ten years of teaching experience. There was definitely something unusual about the way the child was acting. She wondered if there was a diagnosis.

"Can it!" The quavery-but-loud voice came from the cottage on the other side of the one the man and child were apparently going to occupy. "People are trying to sleep!"

Yikes. Mr. Kennedy was cranky enough with ordinary life. He'd chided Gabby about Caramel's barking on multiple occasions. He often complained to Gabby's aunt, who ran the cottage resort, about tourists' revealing swimming attire.

"Sorry," the man called in the direction of Mr. Kennedy's place. He carried Sloane toward the house, fumbling in his pocket and pulling out a phone. "Door code's in here somewhere," he said, scrolling. One arm held Sloane easily, despite her continued struggles. The guy was *strong*.

He found what he was looking for and punched a code into the keypad beside the cottage door.

Gabby hurried over and picked up one of the suitcases he'd set down. She carried it to his front stoop and then went back for the other. Caramel remained in the crook of her arm, panting, watching the proceedings with apparent interest.

Inside the screen door, the man put down the child but

held her firmly by the shoulders. "Thank you," he said, his voice weary. "I'm sorry we woke you up."

"No problem." She considered introducing herself, but decided that could wait. She wished them goodnight and then turned and headed back toward her cottage. Behind her, she heard the door click shut and the noise of the crying child diminished.

She was getting ready to climb into bed again when a thought struck her.

Sloane had said she was seven, which made it likely she was about to start second grade. Gabby was one of two second-grade teachers at the local elementary school.

Hopefully, the man was just here for an end-of-summer vacation. If he was a long-term resident here, as Gabby was, then chances were fifty-fifty that she'd have Sloane in her class.

The morning after his chaotic late-night arrival in Chesapeake Corners, Maryland, Noah located coffee pods in one of his boxes. While the machine spit out his morning addiction, he looked out the kitchen window toward the row of adjoining cottages, and rubbed a hand over his face. Was this move going to be salvation for him and Sloane, or the worst mistake of his life?

The cottage resort was pretty, that was for sure. From what he could see now, and what he'd noticed driving in last night, the place looked to consist of ten or twelve small cottages arranged roughly in a circle. Situated on a spit of land that jutted into the Chesapeake Bay, the cottages surrounded a common area with picnic tables and a playground. The small houses all looked of a similar size: two small bedrooms, a living area and a kitchen.

They were all painted gray with white trim. Each had a front stoop, furnished with rocking chairs. At the back of the homes on his side, open yard space led down to the Chesapeake Bay. At the entrance, a slightly larger cottage with an abundance of flowers had to be the one belonging to the owner-manager, Dee Rhoades.

He'd signed a six-month lease with her. He had to make this work. Sloane's healing and happiness depended on it.

He picked up his coffee and walked out onto the screened back porch that faced the bay. He breathed in the fragrance of salty water and enjoyed the feel of the breeze on his face. A couple of mallards quacked as they skidded into their water landing.

It was beautiful and it was going to inspire him to write, he could already tell. That would make his agent very, very happy.

But first, he had to get himself and Sloane settled. Fortunately, the cottage was furnished, but he needed to unpack their belongings and set up her room, at a minimum. Show her the school and put out feelers for a reputable babysitter and maybe even some easygoing potential playmates.

"Daddy?" Sloane called. Her voice was fearful, and he set down his coffee and went to her room.

She was sitting up in bed, and at the sight of him, her face relaxed into a smile. She stretched and looked around, and his heart filled with an impossible mixture of love and concern.

"Come on out and see our new home," he said. Out of habit, he kept his voice calm and upbeat. Her smile suggested this might be a good day, but then again, transitions were hard for her. He led the way to the kitchen. "We're going to have breakfast and do some unpacking, and then look around town."

"Can we visit my new school?"

"Maybe," he said. "We'll have to see."

Her forehead wrinkled and her eyes narrowed.

"Which do you want, Pop-Tarts or a muffin?" It was a distraction ploy, and it worked.

"Pop-Tarts!" She climbed into a chair at the little kitchen table.

He handed her a foil package to open and found a juice box. "We'll hit the grocery store today, too." He had to get some healthier food for her. For both of them.

"You can't hit a store, Daddy. You're silly." She bit into her Pop-Tarts. "Mmm. This is good."

Relieved that she seemed off to a fairly good start, he tore open a package of Pop-Tarts for himself. He took a bite. Ugh. Grape, frosted, with sprinkles. Yeah, he really needed to get to the store.

"Look, Daddy!" Sloane scrambled out of her chair and went to the window. "It's that lady and her dog! Can we go see her?"

He looked out and spotted their helper from last night. She wore shorts and a sky blue T-shirt, and she was holding her dog's leash while talking on her cell phone.

Her long blond hair was an exact match to Sloane's. She laughed and talked, and his heart skipped a beat.

He watched her as she knelt, her little dog in front of her. Off the phone now, she spoke to the dog, waited for some reaction he couldn't discern, and then gave the dog praise and a treat.

She looked so…wholesome. And she'd been kind last night, helping him get the suitcases in and not complaining about being awakened. Hadn't even seemed judgmental about Sloane's meltdown. Maybe this whole improbable scheme was going to work.

"Can we go see her, Daddy?"

Noah's gut tightened. Might as well get started. "After

we finish breakfast, we can go see her," he told Sloane. "If you're polite and show good manners."

"I will!" Sloane stuffed the rest of her Pop-Tarts pastry into her mouth.

Noah finished his own Pop-Tarts pastry. Not bad, actually. The grape had grown on him. He held out a box of cellophane-wrapped muffins. "Choose one to take to our neighbor. It'll be a nice way to apologize for waking her up last night. Come here," he added, and wiped a streak of grape from her face.

Her eyes narrowed. She didn't like having her face wiped.

"How's my face?" he asked, distracting her. He held out the napkin he'd used on her.

She giggled and wiped a streak onto, not off of, his face. "You're a mess, Daddy!" She laughed harder as he made a game of looking for a mirror to clean himself up.

Their faces finally clean, they went outside, and their neighbor looked up and waved. Her little dog gave one yap and then sat, alert, as they walked closer. Noah studied the woman who might become very, very important to him and to Sloane.

"We want to 'pologize," Sloane said, holding out the muffin on a napkin.

"Say what for," Noah prompted.

"We're sorry we woke you up. Can I pet your dog?"

"She's little, so just pet her gently, with two fingers." She held up two fingers to demonstrate.

As Sloane knelt and carefully petted the little dog's head, Noah smiled at the woman. He wanted to make a good impression. "I'm Noah Barnes, and this is my daughter, Sloane. Sorry we woke you up last night. It was good of you to help with my luggage."

"It's no problem." She extended her hand and he took

it, noting that her skin was soft, her grip firm. "I'm Gabby Dunn. Niece of the owner, Dee Rhoades, so I live here year-round. Are you here for vacation, or longer term?"

"Six months," he said.

"Ah. Do you have friends or family in the area?"

He shook his head. "Just looking for a fresh start."

"It's a good place for one," she said easily. She smiled down at Sloane. "You're doing such a good job of being gentle, honey. I'm about to take my dog for a walk and then I have a meeting at the school."

"Daddy says I can go to my new school and look at it," Sloane said.

Noah liked Gabby's kind attitude toward Sloane. "We have to arrange it with the school, but maybe," Noah said.

Suddenly, Sloane picked up the little dog. She lay on her back and held it above her. Caramel wiggled. Sloane laughed.

"Sloane. Put the dog down." Noah knelt and reached for the dog.

Sloane swung Caramel away from him.

Gabby, on Sloane's other side, bent down and took hold of Caramel. With a deft move, she extracted the little dog from Sloane's hands. "Time for Caramel to leave," she told Sloane. "She helps kids learn to read, and it's time for her appointment."

Sloane sat up and crossed her arms over her chest. "I hate reading."

"Maybe Caramel will help you learn to like it sometime."

Sloane's lower lip stuck out and her eyes narrowed as she studied Gabby. "You're too fat!" she yelled suddenly.

A startled expression crossed Gabby's face, quickly followed by hurt. She turned toward her cottage.

"Sloane!" Flooded with shame and embarrassment, Noah

took his daughter's hand and tugged her firmly to her feet. "We don't talk to people that way."

"Well, she *is*."

"She's not. She's very pretty. And we're going inside for a time-out." Noah was mortified. Gabby had been sweet to them, and this was how Sloane repaid her?

"I'm sorry," he called to Gabby's departing back.

She waved a hand. "Not a problem." She disappeared into her cottage.

But it *was* a problem. He carried a screaming Sloane into the house. "Sit down there. Time-out."

Sloane wailed, but she did stay in the chair he'd designated.

He walked into the kitchen. Sometimes, as much as he loved his daughter, he needed a little distance from her. And since his wife had died a year ago, he'd gotten precious little distance.

The kind of hurtful remark Sloane had just made was a symptom of her oppositional defiant disorder. ODD. Her frequent rages and tantrums were an extreme version of what most young children did occasionally. But the cruel remarks, the purposeful meanness, was different. It was what had led him to seek a diagnosis.

He'd learned that the disorder could be genetic, a difference in the way Sloane's nerves and brain functioned. Since Sloane was adopted and they'd known almost nothing about her birth parents, that was a possibility. But more often, it was the product of a child's environment: a lack of supervision, inconsistent or harsh discipline, abuse, or neglect.

When he'd found that out, it had gutted him. He'd known his wife didn't love being a mom, but he'd learned too late that her discipline was too harsh and that she'd sometimes neglected Sloane's basic needs. She'd been a skillful liar, and that had covered some of her worse actions.

She'd also talked incessantly about losing weight and staying slim, and had made rude comments about other women's bodies. That was probably why Sloane had said Gabby was fat when in fact, the woman's curves were…nice.

Poor Gabby. She barely knew them and had been nothing but helpful. Now, she was probably hoping the next six months would go quickly—and praying that Sloane wasn't going to be in her class.

His hopes of building a good connection with her took a nosedive.

Before gloom completely enveloped him, he called the school and asked if it would be possible for him and Sloane to visit this afternoon.

"Of course! Let me look up her teacher and see if she's in the building. Second grade, you said?"

"Right."

Computer keys clicked, and then the woman came back on the line. "She'll have Mrs. Forsythe as her main teacher. She's not in today, unfortunately. But your daughter will also work on reading with the other second-grade teacher, Miss Dunn. I believe Gabby's planning to come in this afternoon, if you'd like to meet her. I'm sure she'll be fine with a visit."

"Great." Only it wasn't.

He ended the call and sank into a chair at the small kitchen table. He was thankful that Sloane wasn't in Gabby's class, but concerned that his daughter might work with Gabby on her least-favorite subject, reading.

Gabby, who'd been so kind. Gabby, whom his daughter had just rudely insulted.

Gabby, who, unbeknownst to her, was Sloane's birth mother.

Chapter Two

"You seem a little blue," Gabby's friend Angie said to her that afternoon. They were walking toward the school, Gabby to put the finishing touches on her classroom, and Angie to talk to a couple of teachers about therapy dog visits. Beside them, Caramel trotted on her leash.

Angie ran a small nonprofit focused on therapy dogs, and she had helped Gabby get and train Caramel. She was in charge of the school's new Read to Dogs initiative. Gabby and Caramel were the first team in the pilot program.

"Are you bummed out that summer is over?" Angie asked.

Gabby swiped her ID card and they entered the building. "Maybe a little," she said. While Angie checked in at the office, Gabby waved at a couple of other teachers. When they saw Caramel, they stopped to pet and fawn over the little dog.

As she talked with her coworkers, catching up on summer news, Gabby's thoughts wandered to Noah and his daughter. The child clearly had some issues. It wasn't usual for a second grader to make hurtful comments to an adult, at least not to a stranger. Something was up with Sloane.

Gabby tried hard not to be negative about any child. There were all kinds of possible reasons for her rudeness. But she had to admit that comments about her weight hurt.

They shouldn't. She'd long ago made peace with being a

curvy girl. At least mostly. But she didn't love being called fat. It reminded her of teasing she'd experienced in school, and later, sharp criticism and outright mockery from her husband.

Angie emerged from the office. "I see you've met our best advocate for the Read to Dogs program," she said to the teachers who were petting Caramel. She pulled out business cards and handed one to each teacher. "If you want your struggling readers to participate, give me a call. We'll have several dogs visiting the school this year."

The teachers headed on down the hall, and Angie walked beside Gabby to her classroom. There, Gabby let Caramel run around, sniffing everything. The more comfortable she was in this environment, the better it would work.

Twice a week, Caramel would spend a morning or afternoon at school with Gabby, working with the second graders who struggled with reading. They were presenting it as a fun program to be earned through good behavior, making struggling readers feel special in a positive way rather than deficient. It had required some persuasion and some reorganizing of schedules, but they'd made it happen.

"You're going to be my number one success story," Angie said confidently. "It'll be exciting to see how the kids' reading scores improve."

"Let's hope." Gabby set down her things.

Angie stood in the doorway, studying Gabby. "Tell me what's wrong," she said.

Gabby looked around at the gleaming floors, the neatly arranged desks, the colorful bulletin boards. "I just…had a weird encounter. Last night and then this morning." She told her friend about Noah and Sloane's arrival and what Sloane had said.

"Ouch."

"And she might be in my class, but I'm hoping not." Gabby

sighed and perched on the edge of her desk. "I need to let go of it. I can't be oversensitive when I want to adopt a child myself. It's likely that a child from the foster care system would have some challenges. Act out. Say mean things from time to time."

And Gabby had every reason to be open and accepting of any child, given her own background. She had no room to judge.

"That's true, there are some troubled kids in the system," Angie said. She was one of the only people who knew of Gabby's desire to adopt. Gabby had shared it with her because Angie and her husband were in the process of adopting a sibling group themselves. "We've been learning about that in our training sessions. But it's also important to acknowledge your own feelings and take care of yourself. What that little girl said was hurtful." She paused. "But you know what she said isn't true, right? You're gorgeous."

"Thank you. I'm mostly happy with how I look." Gabby knew she wasn't a beauty like Angie, but she was fine. It was what was inside that mattered, anyway.

"Good," Angie said. "We women are under such pressure about looks and weight. I mean, think of Vanessa."

"Exactly. I'm so glad she's getting better." Vanessa, their friend and now Angie's sister-in-law, had struggled with an eating disorder. With the help of counseling and the support of her brother, Angie's husband, Vanessa was becoming healthy and strong.

Angie frowned. "It's too bad a little girl is already thinking about weight. I wonder why?"

Gabby shrugged. "Calling someone fat is a pretty common insult. In fact, that's the kind of thing my ex would always say." Gabby reached down and picked up Caramel, who licked her face and then settled into her arms. Caramel loved to be carried around, and Gabby had to discipline herself to let the dog walk most of the time, so that she could be independent and get some exercise.

"Your ex sounds like a jerk," Angie said.

Gabby snorted. "You don't know the half of it." Memories rose unbidden, cruel words and crueler actions. She shoved them aside and took a couple of deep breaths.

You're done with him. He can't bother you. He hasn't contacted you in years.

In her arms, Caramel looked up at her with concerned, black button eyes.

Angie noticed the time on the big wall clock. "Oh, man. I have to go meet with the upper grade reading specialists. Hang in there, and let's go out soon."

"I'd love to." Although, Gabby knew, Angie didn't have tons of time to go out. She was busy with her new husband, their adoption plans and her therapy dog business.

As Angie walked out, Gabby's principal came down and knocked on the doorjamb. "Would you be able to meet with a new second-grade student and her father? She's not in your class, but we've tentatively placed her in your new reading program."

"Of course," Gabby said, suppressing a sigh. She knew exactly who the new student was going to be.

Noah knelt in front of Sloane, just outside the classroom door. "I expect good behavior," he said. "Do you remember the three things that means?"

"Yes, Daddy." Sloane tossed back her hair and rolled her eyes. With the glittery jeans and snug-fitting T-shirt she'd picked out to wear, she looked like a miniature teenager.

"Tell me what they are," he said. He was pushing her, which didn't always go well, but he really, really wanted sweet Miss Dunn to get a better impression of Sloane. For all kinds of reasons.

"Look people in the eye," she said. "Answer their questions. Don't interrupt."

"Good." There were so many more elements to being a pleasant child, but those three were enough for Sloane to concentrate on. She was in a strange environment and she didn't do well with transitions. Noah was hoping to get through this visit without a meltdown, and without Sloane insulting anyone, especially her new teacher.

"Come on in," the principal said. "I'm leaving you in Miss Dunn's capable hands. Gabby, can you walk them to the parking lot when you've had a chance to visit?"

"Of course." Gabby smiled.

To Noah, her smile looked forced. And no wonder. She'd already had a taste of Sloane's sharp attitude.

But to her credit, she didn't let any negative feelings show. "I'm excited for the school year to start," she said to Sloane. "I hear you might be in my special reading program."

Noah hoped so. He'd heard more about the program from the principal, and it sounded tailor-made for Sloane, who hated reading but liked animals. Noah desperately wanted Sloane to get into reading, and not just because he was a writer who made his living with words. He also knew that reading was a key to success in most school subjects. Even more important, it was a way to escape difficult emotions, or deal with them better. Sloane needed that, badly.

Unfortunately, Sloane tended to resist a lot of things that would be good for her. Defying authority was her thing. Indeed, she opened her mouth as if to speak out against joining the reading program, but then, from a corner of the room, there was a noise. Caramel stood, stretched, shook herself, and trotted over.

Sloane's face lit up. "Your dog is here!"

"That's right," Gabby said. "She'll be in the classroom with us sometimes, so I brought her here to get used to things."

"Just like me," Sloane said.

Gabby smiled. "Just like you. Would you like to pet her?"

Noah was floored that Gabby would allow that, given how Sloane had acted this morning.

"Yeah!" Sloane said. She started toward the dog.

"Wait," Gabby said firmly, stepping in front of her. "There are conditions."

Sloane tipped her head to one side, obviously unsure of the meaning of the word.

"The conditions are that you can't pick her up or hold onto her if she wants to leave, and you can only pet her with two fingers, like we talked about before." She studied Sloane. "Go ahead, sit beside her and show me you understand."

Noah winced. Sloane's ODD meant she disliked rules, often actively fought against them.

After a moment's hesitation, Sloane nodded. "Okay!" She walked over to the dog, sat down beside her, and petted her with two fingers.

Noah closed his eyes for a brief moment.

Maybe this could work. It was clear that Gabby was fantastic at managing kids, and that she didn't get thrown off or hold a grudge when one acted out.

She'd be a great influence for Sloane.

He'd come here, at Dee's instigation, to check out that very thing. He'd wanted to hope, though he hadn't held out much confidence, that Sloane's biological mother could be a mother figure for a child so much in need.

Sloane's oppositional defiant disorder hadn't been there from birth. It had started to show up when she was three, when her adoptive mother, Noah's wife, had tired of marriage and motherhood, and started to neglect her. And there had been a snowball effect. The neglect had worsened Sloane's behavior, and her bad behavior had pushed her mother into punishments that were way too harsh.

Noah had tried to intervene, to help, but he'd been working more than full-time to support their Washington, D.C., lifestyle.

And then had come the fatal car accident, and despite counseling, Sloane's issues had gotten much worse.

Moving to a smaller, more peaceful community was part of Noah's own treatment plan for his daughter. Connecting with her biological mother, should that person prove to be a positive influence, was a next step.

He hadn't done a good enough job of taking care of his daughter. Now, he was trying to remedy that. It looked like, after a rough beginning, he might be off to a good start.

On Thursday night, Noah greeted Dee Rhoades, the manager of the cottage resort. She was also Gabby's aunt, and the person whose enthusiasm had set this whole move into motion. Noah walked outside and sat with her on the front steps of his cottage.

They both glanced next door. Gabby's car wasn't there, which gave them a little freedom to chat. Sloane was inside watching a Disney movie. It was the only break Noah had gotten from her today.

"How's everything going?" Dee asked.

"Pretty well." He told the older woman about visiting the school. "Sloane doesn't have Gabby as a teacher, but she may be in her reading program."

"With the dog?"

"Yes, with the dog."

"Perfect!" Dee lifted her hands as if she were in church. "See, it's all working out. God has a plan."

Noah hoped that was the case. He hadn't expected anything like this to happen when he'd done the DNA kit for Sloane. He'd just hoped to learn something about her history, hoping it would shed light on her issues and how to help her deal with them.

Instead, it had put him in touch with Dee, Sloane's aunt. Their correspondence had turned into phone calls, and Dee had been easy to talk to on some of those late nights when he'd felt so alone. A longtime foster mother with a heart for troubled kids, she'd listened to his concerns about Sloane and had offered advice and sympathy.

When she'd come up with the idea of him and Sloane moving closer, he'd felt desperate enough to jump on it. And then she'd dropped the bombshell: Gabby, Sloane's birth mother, lived in the cottage resort she ran. If Noah moved in to one of the cottages that happened to be vacant, Gabby and Sloane could get to know each other, naturally, and maybe it would lead to a long-term connection they could all embrace.

He'd hesitated, feeling duplicitous to try to connect with Sloane's birth mother when the adoption had been closed. But Dee had been confident that things would work out. The situation that had caused Gabby to place her baby for adoption was in the past. Gabby was a loving person, good with kids, a teacher. She very much wanted a family, and what better start than a second chance with her own biological daughter?

It had seemed like a long shot, a harebrained idea that was unlikely to bear fruit. But now that they were here, he was guardedly optimistic. "I'll tell Gabby the truth soon," he said to Dee, "as soon as things have settled down. I don't like doing this behind her back. But I just felt like I needed to get to know her, and have Sloane get to know her, before broaching the idea of a partnership."

"It makes sense." She glanced back into the house. "Anything you need, settling in?"

"A caregiver," he said promptly. "Sloane will be in school, of course, which will allow me to get my writing done. But I'm going to need someone who can help out when I have errands or need to take a meeting in the evening."

"Or when you need a little time off," Dee said. "That's important. Would you consider hiring me?"

He blinked. "I'd be thrilled if you wanted to care for Sloane, but honestly, why would you? She's not an easy kid."

"I like a challenge," she said. "She's my biological relative, after all. And don't think I'd do it for free. I'd charge the going rate. That way, I'll be able to hire someone to caretake the cottages while I do a Christmas trip this year."

"If you're serious, that would be wonderful," he said. "Let's give it a onetime trial first, though. You don't know how many caregivers she's gone through." That had been part of the problem with his wife. As Sloane had grown more difficult, it had become harder to hire babysitters who would give Bridgette a break.

"We'll set something up," Dee said. "In fact, I'm free tomorrow night, and I happen to know that Gabby is, too. Maybe she could show you around town, give you a little adult time away from your kiddo."

He narrowed his eyes. Was Dee trying to matchmake?

But the thought of an evening with Gabby *was* appealing. "There's no guarantee she'd want to spend time with me," he said. "But I'd love to have an evening to take in the sights at an adult pace. If you're sure you're up for babysitting."

"Honey, I've been taking care of challenging kids since

before you were born. I'm eager to get to know that child, and having another adult in her corner will be good for her, too."

"It will." Noah was seeing more and more what a blessing Dee was, and would continue to be, in his and Sloane's lives.

Darkness was gathering as Gabby's car pulled into the driveway. Noah stood to slip inside, not wanting to overwhelm Gabby with too much of his presence. She'd already dealt with him a couple of times that day and it hadn't been easy. But before he could duck away, Dee waved her arms and beckoned Gabby over.

"I was just telling Noah," she said, "that I'm happy to do some caregiving for Sloane. We're going to do a trial for a couple of hours tomorrow evening, and I'm afraid I've offered you up as a tour guide to help Noah get to know the town."

"Which is of course totally optional," Noah said apologetically. "I don't want to take up too much of your time, and I'm sure you have your own plans."

"Actually, my dinner date canceled." Gabby looked from Dee to Noah and back again.

Who was the dinner date? Noah wondered. Did Gabby have a boyfriend? It was likelier than not. She was so pretty and kind. It was actually surprising that she wasn't married.

"So you'll do it?" Dee asked.

Noah frowned, feeling like he had no say in the matter. Dee's enthusiasm for her own ideas, and for bringing people together, felt overwhelming. But he wasn't sure how to extricate himself. And, looking at Gabby's pretty face, he wasn't sure he wanted to.

"Well… I could do that," Gabby said. "Sure!" She gave him a sunny smile. "We have some nice restaurants on the water, and the boardwalk is small but pretty."

"See?" Dee said. "Gabby's a sweetheart."

Noah was starting to think the same thing. "You're very

kind," he said. "And I'll take you up on it, if you'll let me buy you a good seafood dinner."

Suddenly, she looked a little wary. "That's not necessary."

"No, but it's a good idea," Dee said briskly. "Eating out is expensive on a teacher's salary."

"It is," Gabby said. She bit her lip.

"Just text me a time, and I'll come let Sloane get used to me a bit before you go," Dee said. She strolled off toward her cottage.

Gabby turned to Noah. "Just to be clear," she said, "this isn't a date. I'm glad to be a good neighbor, but that's all."

"Of course," Noah said. He was surprised to find that he felt a little disappointed. Not that he wanted it to be a date, of course, but he didn't like being so definitively shut down.

"Let's meet out here, say at six?" she suggested. "We can walk down to the waterfront and I'll show you some hot spots. Such as they are." She smiled ruefully. "This is nothing like DC. Not a whole lot of nightlife."

"That's just fine," Noah said. And it *was* fine. Good, even. He found himself looking forward to the evening. Not because he was interested in Gabby, or expected it to be a date. It wouldn't. She'd made that clear.

But a nice dinner out without worrying about a mess or a meltdown? He could definitely appreciate that.

Chapter Three

This wasn't so bad.

Gabby took a sip of after-dinner coffee and leaned back in her chair, looking out at the bay. The setting sun had turned the sky into a hazy watercolor of pink and purple and gold. A gentle breeze ruffled her hair and cooled her face. Birds swooped over the water, their calls punctuating the conversations and laughter of diners at the other tables.

Open-air dining was one of Gabby's favorite things to do, but she rarely did it at such a nice restaurant. Like her aunt had said, places like this were hard to afford on a teacher's salary. Especially a teacher who was saving every spare dollar for her goal of adopting a child.

Noah had insisted on treating her at the nicest waterfront restaurant in town in exchange for a tour after dinner. Gabby was definitely getting the better part of the deal. He'd proven to be a charming dinner companion, asking her about living here, about teaching, about using dogs to help kids learn to read. When she'd turned the tables and questioned him about his life, he'd responded with funny stories about living in DC and about the research he did to write his thrillers.

It was friendly. Fun. Relaxed. It might even fit in with her own goals. Social workers in the adoption field looked for prospective parents who had a broad friend base, both men and women. Children needed role models of both genders. Since she taught elementary school, a field dominated by women, Gabby had few male friends.

So this was good. Having a man in her circle of acquaintances would help her be considered to adopt a boy or a girl, which would double her chances of adopting soon.

As they finished their dessert—a chocolate volcano cake to die for—a man approached their table. He wore the white clothes and stained apron of a kitchen worker. He was slightly stooped, the stubble on his face grizzled. His baseball cap read Vietnam Veteran, and there was a visible scar across his cheek.

"Excuse me," he said quietly, looking from the right to the left, "are you Noah Barnes, the author?"

A slight expression of discomfort crossed Noah's face. Apparently, he didn't like being recognized. But he covered his reaction quickly and smiled up at the man. "I am."

From the pocket of his apron, the man produced a battered paperback. "Could you sign it?"

"Armistice Alley!" Noah's eyes widened. "Of course I'll sign it. Not many people have read my first book." He patted his pockets and produced a pen.

"Oh, I've read all of 'em. Bunch of times. You get it right."

Noah paused in the middle of his inscription and looked at the man more closely. "Navy?"

"Uh-huh."

"Me as well." Noah smiled and started to write something more in the book.

"Excuse me, sir, I do apologize." A man of about thirty, in a stylish business suit, approached and nudged his way close to the table, giving the older man a dismissive wave. "Back to the kitchen, please, Stan. Dishes are piling up."

"Sorry, sorry." Stan ducked his head, took his book from

Noah's hands, and turned back to the kitchen, his face reddening.

"I'd like to finish signing his book first." Noah said the words in an uninflected tone that managed to sound completely authoritative. He stared down the manager, one eyebrow lifted.

Stan paused and looked back.

"Of course, of course. Whatever you want, sir. I just didn't want…" He trailed off.

By now, most of the diners around them were watching as Noah walked past the manager to Stan, finished writing a line or two in his book, and shook his hand. "It was a pleasure to meet you."

"Thank you!" The man tucked the yellowed paperback into his pocket, as if he were holding something priceless. "I don't suppose… I mean, would you mind…" He patted his pockets. "Never mind. My phone's in the back."

Noah pulled his phone out of his pocket and turned back to Gabby. "Mind taking a picture?"

"Glad to." She was surprised by Noah's kindness, but she shouldn't have been. He was a thoughtful, compassionate man; she'd seen that from the way he related to Sloane.

Noah and Stan posed, the book held up between them as both men smiled. Gabby took several shots.

"I'll send it to you." Noah pulled out a business card and handed it to Stan. "Just contact me here."

"I will!" After a glance at his manager, Stan hurried back toward the kitchen.

Noah returned to the table but didn't sit. Instead, he faced the manager, his bearing erect. "If he's an example of your staff—" he started.

"He's not—"

"If he's an example of your staff," Noah repeated, not raising his voice, "I'd like to commend you for hiring a veteran. I'm guessing he's a hard worker, as well."

"Oh, he is." The manager stumbled over a few more apologetic phrases before walking away, his expression sheepish.

Gabby looked at Noah with new admiration, and then caught herself. Okay, so he'd been kind to a fan, maybe helped the older man avoid trouble with his boss. Even— from the look on Stan's face—made his day.

That didn't mean she needed to go all fangirl on him. It definitely didn't mean she should be attracted to him. What he'd done was not that big of a deal, was it?

Lots of people were kind and did admirable things. She was going to express her appreciation like she would to anyone. She was definitely *not* going to start thinking about Noah in any kind of a romantic way. She didn't do romance, hadn't for years. She wasn't going to start now.

After Noah had paid the check and they'd left the restaurant, they walked out onto the boardwalk. "That was a good thing you did in there," Gabby said.

"Hope Stan doesn't get in trouble," Noah said. "Kitchen work's a hard job for someone who's probably pushing seventy."

"Your books give him an escape."

"That's my hope."

As they walked, he scrubbed a hand over his face, and Gabby realized the encounter hadn't been easy for him. "You're an introvert," she guessed.

"One hundred percent." He glanced back at the restaurant. "Stuff like that wears me out."

"Do you get recognized often?" she asked, smiling. "Will you have to wear a disguise to our second-grade Doughnuts with Dad event?"

"No." He laughed, too. "I can count on one hand the number of times I was recognized in DC. I'm hoping the same will be the case here, aside from my man, Stan."

"Don't worry," she assured him. "Generally, Chesapeake Corners is a good place to hide."

At least, she'd found it to be so far. There was no reason things should change now. Todd was out of her life for good, thankfully.

A good place to hide?

As they walked along the boardwalk beside the bay, Noah studied Gabby covertly. Did she have something to hide? And if so, was it in any way connected to the fact that she'd had a child and placed her for adoption?

Noah knew there were plenty of reasons why birth mothers couldn't raise their kids. Maybe Gabby had been a single mom and hadn't had the means to raise a child. Maybe there had been a health issue, even a mental health issue.

He was curious about it, and he hoped that eventually he could hear the whole story. But now wasn't the time to ask. It was way, way too soon.

His goal tonight was to get to know Gabby well enough to decide whether to reveal to her the fact that she was Sloane's birth mother. Once he figured that out, he'd know how to move forward.

From what he'd seen of her, he liked Gabby. Respected her, too. She seemed like a great person who'd be a good influence in Sloane's life.

But he'd thought he had known his wife, too, and he'd been sadly mistaken. He'd believed her claim that she wanted to be an adoptive mom. He'd been naive about her lies. Unaware of the fact that she had been breaking her wedding vows.

He couldn't let something like that happen again. Not when

it would have a major impact on Sloane's already-precarious state of mind.

"How many books between *Armistice Alley* and *Imperfect Storm*?" she asked. Then she wrinkled her nose, her face reddening. "I'm sorry. *Imperfect Storm* was the first I heard of you. It's the only one of yours I've read."

"It's okay. There are five books in between. *Storm* is my seventh." Noah was actually surprised she'd even read one of his books. "My books aren't to everyone's taste. Honestly, most civilians aren't keen on all the military details."

"Oh, I loved it. Especially the history."

That made Noah happy. "Thank you for reading it. It was the connection to the news that made it fly off the shelves. To be honest, I wasn't ready for the attention."

"Understandable."

To their left, the bay lapped, gentle and rhythmic, against the rocky shoreline. To their right, beds of large rosebushes made the night air fragrant. They strolled at a slower pace now, and Noah realized he hadn't felt this peaceful in a long time.

But he needed to keep his mind on his goal: vetting Gabby to see if she should be a part of Sloane's life. This wasn't supposed to be a relaxing date. This was business, parenting business.

She gestured toward an information sign beside the path. "Do you know the history of Chesapeake Corners? It's really interesting."

Her enthusiasm made him smile. "No. I actually don't." He paused and squinted, trying to read the sign in the moonlight. "I'll have to come back during the day. It's too dark to read it."

"You should," she said. "Basically, because of its location, it was an important port in three wars. The Revolutionary War, the War of 1812 and the Civil War."

"I should know it, then. Military history is kind of a thing in my books." He'd have to read up on the area. He'd been so focused on Gabby's presence here, and Dee's and the day-to-day amenities for Sloane's well-being that he hadn't given much thought to the history of the region.

"You want to hear more? Or am I boring you?" She tucked a strand of long blond hair behind her ear and looked up at him with big, concerned eyes.

You could never be boring. "Of course not. I'm intrigued."

She gestured toward the opposite end of the park, seeming completely unaware of his male appreciation. "That neighborhood over there is one of the oldest free Black communities in the United States. Even way before slavery ended, we had Black merchants and businesspeople working alongside white merchants. During the 1850s and 1860s, this town was a haven for enslaved people escaping to the north."

"That's impressive. I'd like to learn more about it." Especially if a very pretty, earnest teacher would help him.

"We have a museum," she said promptly, dashing his hopes of a one-on-one tutoring session. "I can point it out to you. It has an excellent collection of history books in the gift shop."

"Great." He was disappointed she didn't seem to want to help him explore the area beyond tonight. But she'd hooked him with her enthusiasm, and he felt a telltale spark of excitement. He liked to include historical and political elements in his books. Maybe Chesapeake Corners was going to be more than a refuge; maybe it would be an inspiration as well.

They reached the end of the boardwalk. An observation area offered benches and a wide railing, and they both walked toward the railing and leaned against it, looking out over the water.

Feathery clouds moved over the moon, changing the look of the bay from shiny to dark and then back again. Somewhere in the undeveloped wetlands to their right, a loon gave a mournful cry.

Noah inhaled the scent of the bay. "Smells like the ocean."

"Right? It's the brackish water. Half fresh, from the rivers that feed in from the north, and half salt water from the ocean end down south."

He smiled, watching her. "You're pretty knowledgeable about the area."

"Was it too much? I tend to geek out on history and science." Her brow wrinkled as she looked up at him.

When their eyes met, he felt his stomach tighten. For a moment, he couldn't look away.

"I liked it," he said finally. It was true. Intellectual curiosity was a big part of his own life and work, but he'd never dated someone who had the same type of interests.

You're not dating her, he reminded himself.

Instead, he needed to focus on the ways her sharp mind could benefit Sloane. Tonight was suggesting to him that Gabby was a good person and that revealing the truth about Sloane would be the right thing to do.

The moon emerged from under the clouds, making her blond hair shine silver. She was still looking up at him, her bright eyes suggesting liveliness and fun.

Noah's heart tugged toward her. Everything in him wanted to put an arm around her, keep her warm, draw her close.

But no. That wasn't happening. He didn't get that vibe from her, and he needed to stifle it in himself. He drew in a breath and let it out again slowly, trying to release the pent-up energy inside him.

He'd take a long, hard run tomorrow morning. He needed to find ways to discharge this type of tension so he could stay focused on what mattered.

Before coming to Chesapeake Corners, he'd thought about what kind of issues might crop up if he told Gabby the truth about her connection with Sloane. What he hadn't anticipated was that feeling romantic toward her would be one of them.

And it wouldn't be, he told himself firmly. Tonight's emotions were just about the moonlight. What mattered was that he tell Gabby the truth, and soon, so that she and Sloane could build a relationship that would benefit both of them.

Chapter Four

On Saturday, after helping her aunt around the cottage resort all morning, Gabby went back to the downtown park
where she'd walked with Noah last night.

It was a completely different place today. Every Labor
Day weekend, Chesapeake Corners hosted Crabfest, and
things were already in full swing. A mix of tourists and local
residents crowded in front of a bandstand, where a country
Western group twanged out popular hits. Sun beat down on
her back, and the fragrance of fried food filled the air.

Fortunately, she'd anticipated the excitement and brought
her carrier for Caramel. It was true that walking was better
for the little dog, both for health and for managing her intense Yorkie energy. Plus, Gabby preferred not to reinforce
the stereotype that Yorkies were decorative toys.

In a crowd, though, the risk was too great that someone
would accidentally trip over—or step on—the little dog. So,
as they approached the crush of people, Gabby picked Caramel up and put her in her sling carrier. "There you go," she
said. "Now, you can see everything that's going on."

Caramel leaned back against Gabby's chest and looked
around with bright eyes, panting a little, her ears relaxed.

Vendors lined the boardwalk, selling everything from
jewelry to soap to flowers. The fragrance of steamed sea-

food and hush puppies made Gabby's mouth water. She'd purposely skipped lunch, knowing how great the food was at Crabfest.

"Miss Dunn!" and "That's my teacher!" rang out from the kids' craft tent, and Gabby went over to greet the students, current and former. She gave and received hugs and spoke with parents. Caramel was a big hit, of course. In fact, it was hard to get away. "Come to the library booth later," she told a couple of last year's students, who were particularly enthralled by the dog. "Caramel would love for you to read with her."

She made her way to the library booth, grabbing a bag of spicy beer-battered crab poppers on the way. By the time she and Caramel had made it through the crowd, the librarian, Miss Bernice, had set up a beanbag chair and pillows to create a reading area for Caramel. A small table held several books of poetry for kids. Read a Poem to a Dog! was written on a sandwich board beside the reading nook.

Gabby shared the crab poppers with Miss Bernice, and set out her own sign of standard instructions for handling dogs. Then she put Caramel on a soft pillow beside the beanbag chair, latching her leash for safety's sake. Caramel was well-trained, but of course she wasn't perfect.

Within minutes, several kids had come over and, after a bit of arguing, formed a line. Gabby pointed out the rules and the stack of kids' poetry books, and got the first child reading. Then she retired to an adult-sized rocking chair six feet away, where she could offer direction and encouragement without too much interference.

"I see you've brought that yappy little dog." The male voice came from her left, behind a shelf of used books for sale. Then a familiar tall, thin man with wispy white hair stepped into her line of vision.

"Hi, Mr. Kennedy." Gabby always tried to be kind to her cranky neighbor. She figured there were reasons why he acted the way he did. And no doubt, a Yorkie's bark could be annoying. "She's part of a program encouraging kids to read."

"When I was young, parents and teachers just sat us down in a chair and handed us a book. We didn't have a choice but to read."

"It's a new day, Paul," Miss Bernice said, looking up from her laptop. "Children aren't the little automatons we were."

"No, they're spoiled and overindulged." Mr. Kennedy glared at Miss Bernice, who glared right back.

"Whatever works to get kids reading," Gabby said, hoping to restore peace. "Are you finding anything you like today, Mr. Kennedy?" A love of reading was the one thing she had in common with the older man.

He held up a copy of *David Copperfield*. "Decided to take another look at this after reading that bestseller based on it."

"Both are great books."

The voice behind Gabby sent a tiny prickle of awareness down her spine. Noah. She'd wondered if he would come to Crabfest today.

"I was thinking the same thing," Noah went on, smiling at Mr. Kennedy. "I'd like to reread Dickens."

An attractive guy who liked to read thick, heavy novels. Wow. Quickly, Gabby introduced Noah and Sloane to Mr. Kennedy, then to Miss Bernice. The three adults dove into a discussion of Dickens and his work while Gabby helped a nervous child settle in to read a poem to Caramel.

When she returned, Sloane was tugging at her father's arm. "Daddy, can I play with Caramel?"

Noah looked in the direction Sloane was pointing. "Looks like she's busy," he said.

"If you want to read to her, you can get in line," Gabby said, smiling at the little girl. It was a new day, and she was determined to find a way to reach her challenging student.

Sloane's lip curled into a sneer. "Reading is for dummies," she said.

Miss Bernice's eyes widened.

Mr. Kennedy frowned at Sloane, his forehead wrinkling. "People who don't read are the dummies, young lady," he said.

Uh-oh.

Sloane propped her hands on her hips, looking up at Mr. Kennedy. "You're an old man," she said. "Really, really old."

To Gabby's surprise, Mr. Kennedy's face broke out into something resembling a smile. "I *am* old," he said. "That's why I'm so smart. I've had time to read a lot of books." He held up his copy of *David Copperfield*.

"We have some other classics over here," Miss Bernice said. "Have you read *Gulliver's Travels*?"

"Of course I have," Mr. Kennedy sputtered. "Every intelligent person is familiar with Jonathan Swift." He looked at Noah, then at Sloane, then back at Noah. "You might enjoy 'A Modest Proposal,'" he suggested, then followed the librarian to a far corner of the tent.

Gabby's eyes widened. "Wait a minute, isn't that the essay where he talks about eating kids as a food source?"

Noah was chuckling. "Yes. Satirical, and I'm sure Mr. Kennedy wasn't taking it seriously."

"Of course not." But Gabby couldn't help laughing. "He's a character, all right."

"What's so funny?" Sloane asked.

"Mr. Kennedy has some interesting book recommendations," he said.

"Books," Sloane huffed out, rolling her eyes.

"There are some free books for kids," Gabby offered. She

pointed at a table that held gently used kids' books. "One per customer, I think."

"That's right," Miss Bernice said, coming back over. "Look through and see if anything strikes your fancy."

Gabby took the opportunity to tell the librarian that Noah was an author. It turned out she'd read several of his books, and they launched into a discussion while Gabby checked on Caramel and the line of kids waiting to read to the dog.

When she came back over, she heard Miss Bernice saying, "Maybe after you've settled in, we could get you to give a talk at the library."

"It's possible," Noah said. "I'm a big fan of libraries."

Gabby smiled to herself. Miss Bernice was very persuasive, especially for the good of the library. She was pretty sure Noah would be doing a talk within the month.

Sloane was pawing through the free books. One of them, called *My Mom's a Firefighter*, seemed to attract her interest. Then she shoved it aside. "I hate reading," she said.

"Her attitude toward reading must be hard for you," the librarian said to Noah. "Since books and writing are so much a part of your life."

"That's the least of my problems." Noah sounded weary.

"We'll work on reading this year," Gabby promised. "We really value it at CC Elementary, and we do our best to make it fun. Not many second graders escape without learning to love books."

Noah and Sloane soon left the tent, and after another half hour of letting the kids read to Caramel, Gabby closed down the station and put Caramel back into her carrier. The dog was eager and would work until she was exhausted, but it wasn't good to push her limits. Anyway, the Labor Day parade was about to start.

"Thanks so much for doing this today," the librarian said

to Gabby. "You're always such a wonderful advocate for reading."

"Caramel's the best advocate," Gabby said, rubbing the little dog's ears. "We'll watch the parade for a little bit, and then go home for a nap."

As Gabby walked toward the parade route, a block down from the starting area where the high school band was warming up, she heard a small, sweet voice. "Miss Dunn. Come sit with us."

It was Sloane, sitting beside her father on the wall of a long concrete planter. And maybe she was only being sweet because Gabby was carrying Caramel, in a cute sling no less, but it was a side of her Gabby hadn't seen before.

She glanced at Noah's face. His eyebrows were up, his chin dipped, as if he was surprised, too.

If this was an overture of friendship, Gabby wasn't going to ignore it. Sloane needed all the encouragement she could get. She walked over and sat beside the little girl.

Leading the parade was a float celebrating crabbers, the main laborers in the area. It featured a giant crab with legs that moved, and crabbers dressed in their work gear tossed plastic crabs and candy to the kids.

More groups went by, a pipe-and-drum corps, troops of scouts, and floats advertising local businesses. Gabby set Caramel on the grass, secured with her leash, and Sloane petted the dog's head with two careful fingers. A younger boy, maybe three or four, came over and watched, and soon Sloane was explaining the two-finger rule and the fact that Caramel helped kids learn to read.

Huh. The child was behaving well, taking the rules seriously.

Noah was watching the high school band march by, his toe tapping. "Did you play an instrument when you were younger?" Gabby asked, watching to make sure the little boy was gentle with Caramel.

"I did," Noah said after the loudest section of the band had moved down the street. "Trumpet."

"Throughout high school, or longer? Do you still play?"

He smiled. "I played through college, but when I joined the navy, I let it go."

"Sounds like you regret it."

He shrugged. "Somewhat, but the Navy was kind of a family tradition. My dad was career military."

"Ah." That put a different perspective onto Noah. "He must be proud of you."

Noah glanced down at Sloane, who was busily chatting with the little boy. Then he spoke quietly, over the children's heads. "No, I wouldn't say he's proud."

"Why not? You served, you're a bestselling author..."

He shook his head. "I left the service early. Didn't make a career of it, like my father and grandfather did. Instead, I became a writer. Married a woman not vetted by Mom and Dad and—" his voice lowered to an almost-whisper "—adopted a child whose behavior can be...interesting. No, I wouldn't say either of my parents are proud."

Sympathy washed over Gabby. "Are you close now?"

He shook his head. "They retired out to Arizona, and I see them once a year. They have friends out there, longtime military friends. They seem happy."

"Any brothers or sisters?"

He shook his head. "I was an only child."

Gabby glanced down, ensuring that Sloane was still occupied. She gave a slight downward nod toward the child. "Is her mom part of her life?"

He hesitated, then spoke quietly. "That's a story for another time."

She was surprised by the little spark of excitement inside her. It wasn't about hearing the story of Sloane's mom, although that did interest her. No, she was excited by the idea that there might be *another time* for telling the story of Sloane's mom. It suggested that he wanted, or expected, to see her again.

Probably just because they were neighbors, or because Sloane was in her class. It was inevitable that they'd spend some time together. And the last thing Gabby needed was to get overly enthusiastic about Noah. He was the parent of her student, and that was all.

The more important takeaway from their conversation was that Noah didn't have any family support. From what she could see, he was dealing with a difficult situation on his own.

A team of gymnasts passed in front of them in matching green-and-black leotards. They were all ages, from tiny tots to teens, and they cartwheeled and leaped. "That's my granddaughter," someone yelled.

A passing clown made faces at kids, then handed them pieces of candy. A group of commercial fishermen rode a float shaped like a fishing boat, earning applause and cheers.

Gabby would have expected a sophisticated city guy like Noah to be quickly bored by their small-town festivities. But to her surprise, Noah seemed to enjoy the parade, even the highly unskilled barbershop quartet and the local politician who rode in an open convertible that sported insulting signs about his opposition.

Sloane tugged on Gabby's sleeve. "Miss Dunn! This boy petted Caramel with *three* fingers!" She pointed at the boy she'd been instructing earlier.

The boy's face scrunched up like he was about to cry. "I'm sorry," he said, covering his face with his hands.

"It's okay," Sloane said. "You can try again. Can't he, Miss Gabby?"

Gabby was encouraged by this sign of Sloane's sweeter side. "Of course. Everyone gets a second chance."

The little boy petted Caramel, cautious under Sloane's watchful eye, as Noah watched, too. His hand went down to stroke Sloane's hair, very lightly. The little girl shifted to lean against his legs.

At that moment, they were just any father and daughter enjoying a small-town parade. It touched Gabby's heart.

Which it wasn't supposed to do. She wasn't supposed to be sitting here with Noah and Sloane. She was supposed to be relaxing, getting mentally prepared for school to start on Tuesday.

And since her goal was to adopt a child herself, and not get romantically involved with any man—especially her neighbor, who was also the father of a new student at her school—she needed to stop. Now.

"I think I'm going to head home," she said. "Caramel and I are tired."

Noah wanted to cry out *No! Don't go!*

He'd been enjoying the small-town parade. Enjoying Gabby's company, too. But he was also thinking tonight would be a good night to tell Gabby the truth. If she left without them, that possibility would be closed off.

Sloane was having trouble restraining a yawn. When he suggested that they go home, too, she didn't argue.

Using good manners and controlling her feelings in a crowd hard tasks for his daughter, and she'd done well today. "We can come back tomorrow if we feel like it," he told her, "for the boat races and fireworks."

She nodded, perking up when she realized that Gabby and

Caramel would walk with them. The three of them strolled together, slowly, Gabby carrying Caramel in her sling. The sun was setting over the bay as they left the park, white clouds punctuating the sky's purple and orange and gold. A gentle breeze blew away the heat of the day.

Noah wished, way too much, that this were a simple walk with a beautiful woman. A beautiful, kind, intelligent woman he'd like to know better.

His feelings were getting involved. He needed to stifle that.

Sloane reached up and took Gabby's hand. Gabby smiled down at Sloane.

Yeah. Sloane's feelings were getting involved, too.

Okay then. He sucked in a breath and straightened his back.

He needed to let them both know the truth. Gabby's aunt had said she'd be glad to be there for any discussions, since she'd been involved in making the connection between them. That might be a good idea, he thought, especially when the truth was revealed to Sloane.

Gabby, though…he found he wanted to tell her himself, and soon. That had to be the first step.

If she decided she didn't want to be involved—which was her right—then they needed to leave Sloane out of the loop, entirely.

They walked through quiet streets. A few porches held families or small groups, most talking quietly, a couple louder party-type gatherings. They passed another family, Mom pushing a stroller, Dad carrying a little one on his shoulders.

Another family. But he and Gabby and Sloane weren't a family, and he needed to remember that.

This was complicated. Rather than getting carried away

with Dee's enthusiasm for getting them all together, he probably should have done the normal thing and written to Gabby via her social worker. Checked on whether she wanted involvement or not.

He hadn't done that, afraid she'd shut down the idea entirely. Or that she'd turn out to be a bad influence. Or that she'd agree to meet and then, seeing Sloane and her issues, would turn tail and run.

The truth was, Gabby might still turn tail and run. She'd seen Sloane's behavior problems firsthand.

He was pretty sure, though, after spending time with Gabby, that she'd agree to some level of involvement with Sloane. Still, walking through the peaceful, tree-lined streets, he was nervous.

They reached the cottage resort. Some tourists were in front of their cottages, music playing as they shared food and drink and talk. A few people were taking walks, including a family with a big standard poodle that caught wind of Caramel in her carrier and gave a quick, sharp bark.

Caramel must have been tired. She didn't even bark back.

When they reached their own little section, all the lights were out, except for a single one in the back room of Mr. Kennedy's place. It was dark enough now that Noah felt like he, Sloane and Gabby were enclosed in their own little cocoon.

They reached his cottage first. He sucked in a breath and spoke before he lost his nerve. "Will you wait while I put her to bed? There's something I want to talk to you about."

"Sure," she said, her expression curious. "I'll put Caramel away and then come back."

He couldn't chicken out now.

Sloane was practically sleepwalking, so he picked her up and carried her to her bedroom. He laid her in bed and tucked the new, bright red stuffed crab he'd bought her on one side of her, and her well-loved teddy bear on her other side. He pulled up the covers and kissed her forehead.

"Love you, Daddy," she said, her voice sleepy.

"Love you too, muffin. So much." He sat down on her bed and stroked her arm until she fell asleep just a minute later.

He would have liked to go to bed himself. Or read a book. Watch TV. Anything but confront the birth mother of his child. It wasn't going to be an easy conversation. Gabby might well get angry at all he'd done behind her back.

But fatherhood wasn't about what you wanted to do, it was about what was best for your child. And the longer he waited, the more likely that Gabby would feel deceived. "This is for you, kiddo," he said in a low voice, careful not to wake her. "I hope it's the right thing to do."

When he went outside, Gabby was already sitting on the steps. He sat down beside her and handed her a soda he'd grabbed.

Her blond hair glinted in the porch light. The sounds—music on the next street over, a few cars passing by—seemed distant now.

He wished this conversation were just a pleasant chat about the festival or the school year. He wished he were coming out here to talk about anything else but what he was going to talk to her about.

Toughen up, he told himself. Then he realized he hadn't planned quite how to tell her.

So he did what he did best. "Can I tell you a story?" he asked.

"Um…sure," she said. She smiled at him, her face serene, accepting. "You're the master storyteller."

"Thanks, but not really," he said. "This story is a true

one. About ten years ago, I got married. I'd always wanted a family, a bunch of kids."

She nodded. "I can relate."

That was interesting, given she'd placed a child for adoption. He pushed on. "It turned out, though, that my wife didn't want to ruin her figure with a pregnancy."

Gabby's eyebrows shot up. "Didn't want to ruin her *figure*?"

Noah had reacted badly to his wife's reasoning at first, too. But he'd come to understand it, or at least, he'd tried his best. "It sounds worse than it was. She was a model, and her slender figure was her livelihood."

"I see." Gabby looked thoughtful, like she was trying to understand.

Noah knew in a flash that she would never have put her figure above having kids.

"I suggested that we adopt," he went on. "She agreed to it, and that's what we did."

Gabby sighed. "I want to adopt one day," she said. "It's a wonderful way to form a family."

"It is," he agreed, surprised. Her perspective wasn't one he'd expect from a woman who'd placed her own child for adoption. He filed away the fact that she wanted to adopt for future reference. Maybe that meant she'd welcome Sloane into her life.

She looked over at him. "So what's next in the story?" she asked. "You've got me curious."

"Right. Good." He sucked in a breath. "It turned out that my wife wasn't an enthusiastic mom. Especially when our baby wasn't easy."

"Sloane." She frowned. "Was she volatile from her infancy, then?"

He tilted a flat hand from side to side. "Somewhat. She cried a lot, but I thought that was just what babies did. I thought she was wonderful, but my wife found her hard to manage. She started leaving Sloane with sitters. Putting her down for naps and letting her 'cry it out,' as she said. By the time Sloane was three, Bridgette neglected and ignored her way too often."

Gabby's eyes widened, and her mouth dropped open. She shook her head. "Wow. How awful." She paused, then asked, "Were you…around? Able to mitigate some of that?"

"Some, but it's the biggest regret of my life that I didn't do more," he said. "I did what I could, but I was preoccupied with building up my writing career to make more money for our family. Doing appearances, hawking my books on any radio or news show that would have me, writing the next book so I could release it quickly. It was the division of labor we'd agreed on. She wanted me to succeed, because she loved our lifestyle. But I should have seen more quickly that things at home were going south." He swallowed hard. None of this reflected well on him. What would Gabby think when she learned it was her own biological child who'd been neglected?

She bit her lip. "It's a hard time in a marriage, having a young child."

"It is." He sighed. "We'd just started counseling, and I told my publisher I'd need to extend my deadline and cancel most of my appearances. Then, my wife died."

Gabby gasped, her hand rising to cover her mouth. "What happened?"

"One-car accident. She hit a tree at a high speed. She'd been drinking." Sudden anger surprised him, red and hot. Bridgette had basically abandoned him and Sloane one final time when she'd gotten into that car intoxicated.

A better person would have focused on how desperate she must have felt. She'd basically taken her own life; she'd just used a car to do it.

But he'd seen the pain in Sloane's eyes when he'd told her that Mommy was gone. He'd held her and wiped her tears. He'd experienced firsthand how her behavior had deteriorated.

As ineffective and irresponsible as Bridgette had been, Sloane had loved her. Kids always loved their parents, no matter how lacking. That was what Sloane's therapist had told him.

Gabby reached out and touched him on the arm. "I'm so sorry."

Noah wanted to relax in her sympathy and enjoy her touch. But he didn't dare. He needed to get on with the story, even though this might be the last moment Gabby was cordial with him.

"After losing her mom, Sloane went out of control. We've had counseling, lots of advice, but at the end of the day she needs a maternal figure."

"I can see that." She looked puzzled, though. She had to wonder why he was telling her this.

And here it came, the part that was going to truly freak her out.

"I was up late one night, scrolling for ideas, and an ad for a DNA kit showed up. I wondered whether some of Sloane's problems might be genetic, so I took her samples and sent them in."

"Oh, wow. What did you find out?"

"Actually," he said, "I was contacted by one of Sloane's relatives." He sucked in a deep breath. "It was Dee. Your aunt."

Gabby looked at him quickly, frowning, and then stared down at the ground, arms crossed, holding her shoulders.

Noah forced himself to wait. To let her reaction come, whatever it might be.

Finally, she met his eyes again. "My aunt is Sloane's blood relative?" she whispered.

A bird perched in a tree, offering up a night song. The fragrance of night-blooming flowers wafted to them, sweet and soft.

He could tell from her expression that she was already half understanding the truth, and there was no point in drawing this out. "She is, Gabby," he said. "There's no easy way to say this, but so are you. You're her relative, too, because... Sloane is the baby you placed for adoption almost eight years ago."

Chapter Five

Gabby stared at Noah as her whole world spun on its axis, landing her in a place she'd never been before.

A place she'd never expected to be. She'd wondered where he was going with his rambling talk but…surely she'd misunderstood. Her skin was tingling, and her heart raced. "Did you say Sloane is…mine?"

"Yes. I'm sorry to spring it on you this way but—"

"How could this happen?" she interrupted. Her head spun with the news, the implications, the feelings. "This isn't supposed to happen."

"I know. I…this has to be hard for you."

"Hard for me?" Gabby buried her face in her hands. She wasn't crying. She was actually half-sick. Queasy. "I think… I might…pass out."

"Put your head between your knees." He put a hand on her back and pressed forward, gently. "It'll help."

She did as he'd suggested, but nothing could help.

The deep wound she'd incurred when she had placed her beloved baby for adoption had taken years to heal. She'd comforted herself by imagining her little girl growing up secure and happy, with well-adjusted parents and friends, a sunny backyard to play in, safe from harm.

Now Noah was saying…what? She turned her face to look at him, resting her head on her knees. "Are you sure?"

"I'm sure." He paused, then spoke again. "I hoped having her birth mother in her life would help her. After meeting you, I'm sure it will. Or at least, it could."

Gabby was already adjusting her mental framework, shifting it away from the sweet, faceless child with the idyllic suburban life and focusing instead on Sloane.

A real kid. A real, troubled kid who was traumatized enough that her adoptive father had gone to desperate measures to try and help her.

Random implications rained down on her. She sat up and wrapped her arms around herself. "You're springing this on me now, right before the school year starts, and she's a student at my school."

"That could just be temporary—"

She ignored him as more potential consequences crashed into her mind. "Don't you see, Noah? There were reasons for the closed adoption. Reasons why I never told anyone. And now you're just casually showing up here, saying 'Here's your daughter'?"

A trembling started deep inside her. If Noah had so casually broken the code of the closed adoption… She looked at the window of the room she knew was Sloane's and cold fear gripped her. She sank to her knees in front of Noah. "Please, please, please don't let anyone else know about this. If her birth father found out…this is for her safety. The closed adoption was for her safety, and now you've…"

"Gabby. It's okay. We can talk about it. I'm not going to tell anyone without your consent."

His calm tone infuriated her. "You come in here and disrupt a little girl's life, and *my* life, and now *you're* acting like the reasonable one?" She felt like throwing things, hitting him.

Around the edges of her shock and fear and anger, something else shone. This new notion of being able to know her little girl whom she'd given up as lost to her forever. It felt something like joy, but it also felt like it could be ripped away from her, leaving her in worse pain than ever. And most terrible of all, it could damage Sloane. Emotionally. Even physically, if the truth got out. "I've got to be alone."

"Understood." He stood and walked beside her as she hurried toward her cottage, his long legs easily keeping up with her. "We'll talk. Your secret is safe. You don't have to be involved at all if you don't want to, but I hope—"

"Goodnight, Noah." She went into her cottage and shut the door behind her, ignoring the distressed expression on his face.

So she hadn't reacted the way he'd thought she should. Fine, fine. Who cared what he thought? The adoptive father of the child she'd never stopped loving but had never known.

Beneath the shock and the anger, something else rose inside her. Something slick and uncomfortable, something that made her want to cringe and hide, like a small child who'd done something wrong.

She'd never expected her child, and her child's adoptive parent, to come and find her. Never thought she'd see her baby again. She'd been able to hide behind a closed adoption and the illusion that placing her child with another family, one carefully vetted by social workers, would be the morally correct thing to do.

Now she had to face them both, the child she'd let go and the man who'd raised her. And it was painful. *So* painful. She'd wanted to raise her daughter, desperately. The pain of kissing her newborn baby goodbye, of letting the nurse and social worker carry her away, had brought such darkness to her heart that she hadn't known how she could continue.

Her faith had gotten her through that awful time. She'd thought it was over.

Now, she had to face it again, with the new knowledge that things had gone horribly wrong for that sweet baby she'd loved too much to keep.

Her back against the door, she slid down until she was sitting on the floor, and wept.

Some survival instinct dragged Gabby out of bed the next day, made her comb her hair and put on a dress and go to church. There, she sat in services only half-conscious of what was going on, barely managing to stand when others did, unable to restrain the tears that kept springing to her eyes.

She couldn't think. She could only feel, but what she felt was an impossible mix of joy and sadness, confusion and fear.

Heaviest was the fear. She needed to talk to Noah and impress on him that this information—her connection to Sloane—could never, ever become public knowledge.

As soon as the service ended, Gabby's friend Angie tapped her on the shoulder. "We're hosting Lemonade on the Lawn today, remember?"

"Oh, no." Gabby's voice sounded rusty and hoarse to her own ears. "I forgot. My cookies are at home."

Angie came around the pew and sat down next to Gabby. She studied Gabby's face. "Don't worry about the cookies. I have plenty and it's raining anyway, so most people won't linger. I can do it by myself if you aren't up to it."

Was Gabby up to it? No, but she wasn't up to anything. "I can help," she said. She stood and pushed back her hair.

"Although I might scare people away. No time for makeup this morning."

"You look fine," Angie said kindly. She took Gabby's arm and steered her toward the church kitchen. They fetched urns of lemonade and coffee, and Angie's large container of cookies, and then headed for the church's covered porch. There, they quickly set up a table out of reach of the steady drizzle that slanted in at the edges of the porch. They put out plates and cups.

A small crowd gathered, and Gabby busied herself serving drinks. She left most of the greeting and talking to Angie. As the crowd thinned, she forced herself to smile and chat a little. Tried to think of others and remember there was a bigger picture. Tried to feel some of God's love and grace and channel it to others.

She felt raw inside, though. Her emotions bounced from one extreme to another. There were intense flashes of joy that, against all expectations, she could see and know the daughter she'd placed for adoption a few days after birth. That quirky, difficult, adorable Sloane was her daughter.

There was worry as she took ownership of the fact that Sloane was a troubled little girl who needed help. Over all of that was fear. Fear of Todd and what he might do if he found out where Sloane was and that she and Gabby were in contact.

When only a few parishioners remained, talking with the pastor, Angie touched Gabby's arm. "Do you want to talk about it?"

"It's that obvious?"

"Yep."

Did she want to talk about it?

What Gabby wanted to do was to survive last night's revelations without completely losing it. Well, here she was, upright, walking and talking. Next, she had to figure out how to handle it and what to do, while prioritizing Sloane's safety and well-being. "Did you ever have something from the past come back to haunt you?" she asked Angie.

Angie raised an eyebrow. "As a matter of fact, yes," she said. Her eyes flickered to someone behind Gabby. "Hi, Mr. Kennedy."

The older man took a couple of cookies and stood between the pair of them, drinking a glass of lemonade. Gabby pushed away her impatience and cast about for a topic of conversation. "How are you liking *David Copperfield*?" she asked finally.

"Humph," he said. "I was trying to read last night, but people were talking. Late and loud." He gave her a meaningful glare.

Had he overheard her conversation with Noah?

"Work out your problems, young lady," he said. He plunked down his glass and left, cookies in hand.

"The plot thickens," Angie said. She glanced around. "I think most everyone's gone home. Tell me what's got you so upset."

So Gabby did. She lowered her voice as she explained that she'd had a baby and placed her for adoption. It was the part she was most ashamed of, the part Angie was likely to judge.

But she didn't. She just hugged Gabby. "How hard that must have been," she said. "Especially knowing how much you love kids."

"It was for safety," she said. "My ex was…is…a violent, abusive man. No baby or child would be safe with him. I couldn't keep my baby safe and I knew it."

Angie stifled a gasp and then hugged Gabby. "I'm so, so sorry. That must have been just awful."

The sympathy nearly undid Gabby. She'd so rarely told

her story that she was most accustomed to the voices in her own head, questioning and often condemning her decision. To have a friend hear the story and offer only acceptance... it was balm to Gabby's aching heart.

Angie stepped back and studied her. "You've been wanting to adopt," she said tentatively. "Any chance you could, I don't know, adopt Sloane back?"

Become Sloane's mom again, for real this time? The idea of it swept through Gabby's chest like a beautiful breeze, but thoughts of her ex quickly blocked that. "I don't think so. I surrendered all my rights. She has an adoptive father, a good one."

Angie nodded. "But it sounds to me like he wants to co-parent. Kind of like what we're doing with Declan."

"Oh, of course that's why you understand." Angie had learned a horrifying secret just a couple of years ago. She'd ended up marrying the uncle of the child her late husband had conceived out of wedlock. Now, she spent a lot of time with the child, helping to raise him.

Not many women could have accepted and embraced her husband's child by another woman. Angie hadn't had an easy time of it. But out of love for the child and for her new husband, Declan's uncle, she'd overcome her pain. Maybe that was why she seemed to glow with peace and happiness these days.

Angie smiled. "God can turn any trouble into joy," she said, with such pure serenity on her face that Gabby was in awe. "If you want to help raise your child, it sounds like you have the opportunity to do it."

A great longing rose in Gabby then. She could be a mother. She *was* a mother, but here was a chance to mother the child she'd borne in so much love and placed for adoption out of fear.

And then a picture of Todd rose up in her, face ugly with rage, fists ruthless, spouting cruel, crushing insults. "I can't. I'm afraid it would come out and my ex would come after me—and worse, after Sloane."

"How could he? He's all the way out in Montana or Colorado, isn't he? Does he even know where you live?"

"He's in Montana," she said, "but he's smart. If he were angry enough, he could find me. Find us."

Angie's face twisted with sympathy. "Oh, honey. That must be so hard to deal with. I'm sure you're torn up inside."

"I am. I'm upset and excited at the same time. I don't know how to feel."

"Of course you don't." Angie put an arm around her. "You've had a huge bomb dropped on you. You've got to be reeling, but remember, you're not in this alone."

Gabby took a deep breath and let it out in a sigh. She did feel a little better after talking with Angie. "Thank you so much. For listening. And for being kind."

"Of course," Angie said. "I'm always glad to listen, but that's not what I meant. You're not in this alone, because God's got this." She gripped Gabby's hand, looked around to make sure they were alone, and bowed her head. "Father, please be with Angie. Protect her and Sloane. And Noah. Show them the right way forward."

Gabby's throat was too tight to speak. So she added her own wordless prayer to Angie's.

As they cleaned up, Gabby thanked Angie again. "You could have judged me, and you didn't. Thank you for being such a good friend."

"You're welcome." Angie gave her a quick hug, then spoke again. "You know, you're going to have to talk to Noah more. And soon."

That thought made a mass of butterflies flock and swirl

in Gabby's chest. This was happening. It was going to move forward; everything was going to change.

She felt a sudden longing to go back to the moment before she'd learned the truth about Sloane. Before Noah had exploded her entire life.

"When are you going to set that up?" Angie persisted.

Gabby puffed out a breath. "I'm so mad at him. I can't believe he did this."

"I get that," Angie said. "Closed adoptions are supposed to stay closed. But yours didn't. So you have to talk to him and figure out what to do, for Sloane's sake at least."

"I guess." Gabby tossed the last few paper cups in the garbage can and started wheeling it into the church kitchen.

Talking to Noah was the last thing she wanted. She had no idea how to start or what to say.

And yet it had to happen, and she knew it.

Noah didn't see or speak with Gabby all day Sunday. He wished he'd thought to set up another time to talk, but she'd departed so quickly after learning the news. He debated whether to call or go over, then decided to let her set the pace. Except…school was starting on Tuesday, and that meant Gabby would have more contact than before with Sloane. He wanted—needed—to know how she intended to treat Sloane, given what she'd just learned.

He was relieved to have told Gabby the truth, but was concerned about her reaction. Somewhere inside, he'd hoped she would embrace the relationship and immediately want to get to know Sloane as a daughter. Of course that wasn't something he could expect.

But despite everything, he'd still found her reaction odd. She'd been so vehement about keeping everything secret, which wasn't what he'd expected. Not after getting to know her. She didn't seem to be the type of person who panicked over other people's opinions of her. On the other hand, she'd mentioned that the secrecy was to keep Sloane safe. He didn't know what to make of that.

He spent Sunday ruminating on all of it, only belatedly realizing he should have immediately found a church for him and Sloane to attend. He needed to worship and hear scripture and gain some wisdom, more wisdom than he could command himself. Sloane, too, needed a spiritual home. He wanted her to meet other children, and Sunday school seemed like it would be a safe place.

But he hadn't done it. A mistake on his part.

As the day went on, he began to question his whole decision-making process. Had he done the right thing, blundering in here on Aunt Dee's whim, trying to force a relationship between Sloane and Gabby?

After all, closed adoptions were closed for a reason. It wasn't a common choice these days, and birth mothers who made that choice had reasons for it. They didn't deserve to have their decisions negated.

What if Gabby wanted him and Sloane out of her life? It would be her right, and he'd have to respect it.

The thought of going back to DC, though, was downright depressing. It would be more of the same untenable situation: Sloane's behavior deteriorating by the day, him trying to help her and not succeeding, and the resultant hit to his creative process putting their livelihood at risk.

His mind gyrated like a carnival ride, going in circles with no end in sight, making him feel a little sick. He went through the motions of the day, cooking Sloane pancakes for both breakfast and dinner, doing their laundry, and making a weak attempt to clean the cottage. He even played Barbies with Sloane, or tried to.

But after he spaced out one time too many, and then tried to make up for it by speaking for one of the dolls in a high, squeaky voice, Sloane rolled her eyes and grabbed a hand-held game to play instead.

Monday was Labor Day, and they'd been invited to a cookout at Gabby's aunt's place. Of course, Gabby would be invited too. Should they still go, or stay home to avoid upsetting her further?

He got his answer when Sloane came bounding down the stairs at 7:00 a.m., wearing red, white and blue, eager to go to the picnic. Sloane must have overheard that there would be a couple other kids her age there. Although her anger issues had sometimes cost her friends back home, she seemed ready to start anew.

He wanted that, too. Besides, what else were they going to do today? Shop the Labor Day sales for school clothes? Play more Barbies?

Since he had to confront Gabby at some point, sooner was probably better than later. And maybe the presence of Gabby's aunt would help ease the friction between them, or at least help them to deal with it.

After a morning spent dealing with Sloane's impatience and her requests to visit Gabby and Caramel—requests he deflected with TV and unhealthy snacks—he and Sloane strolled through the cottage resort, heading for the picnic. Various families were outside, enjoying the holiday in the common picnic area, cooking out or tossing a ball around or playing cornhole. But the biggest noise came from Dee's place, where kids slid on a backyard waterslide, screaming their excitement. Classic rock blared from hidden speakers, and the smell of grilled meat filled the air.

"Looks like we should have brought your bathing suit," he said to Sloane.

"I wore it under my clothes! Miss Dee said to." She pulled up her shirt to reveal her bright red one-piece.

"Way to go." He patted her shoulder.

Dee hurried over to greet them. "I'm glad you came," she said, treating them both to hugs. "There's a food table along the side of the house, and I've enlisted Mr. Kennedy at the grill."

Noah looked over to see the older man carefully turning something over—bratwurst?—that smelled delicious.

"Hey, Jennifer," Dee called, beckoning to a woman and child, both redheads. "Come on over. Someone I want you to meet."

The pair joined them, the little girl running ahead of her mom. She stopped directly in front of Sloane. "I'm Penelope," she said. "What grade are you in?"

Sloane held up two fingers, apparently stricken with shyness.

"Me, too. I'm going to be your friend. Come on." She held out a hand, and Sloane blinked and let herself be led away.

"Sorry." Jennifer laughed and shrugged. "Penelope has a lot of, shall we say, leadership qualities. I can tell her to back off."

"It seems to be working," Noah said, watching as Penelope led Sloane toward the waterslide, a long, blue one powered by a garden hose.

While Dee and the mom talked, Noah looked around the gathering. He wasn't intentionally seeking Gabby out, but the moment he saw her, he felt a strong instinct to go to her.

She looked shell-shocked, her face pale and lacking its usual open smile, her shoulders a little hunched as if she wanted to protect herself. He'd caused that. When he took a step toward her, though, she turned away and disappeared into the crowd.

Well, okay then. "I'm going to help Mr. Kennedy with the grilling," he said to Dee, and headed toward the smell of barbecued chicken and bratwurst. There were enough people here that it would be fairly easy to keep his distance from Gabby, and apparently, that was how they were going to play this party.

Sloane seemed to be having a blast. As he watched her run, leap and skim along the waterslide, following Penelope's lead, he decided she was doing fine. He went to Mr. Kennedy and followed the man's detailed instructions on which spices to fetch and how to baste the chicken breasts with melted butter.

When there was a lull, Mr. Kennedy regarded him with a frown. "I hear you're a writer," he said.

Noah nodded. "I write thrillers."

Mr. Kennedy snorted. "Why would you do that when you could write real novels?"

The sparkle in the older man's eyes suggested he was baiting Noah. Okay, he'd play. "Charles Dickens and William Shakespeare wrote stories that were considered lowbrow in their day."

"You put yourself in that category, do you?" Mr. Kennedy used a long-handled spatula to flip the chicken breasts.

Noah laughed. "Not at all. But it does pay the bills." He surveyed the gathering and noticed that Gabby and her aunt were having a discussion. It looked to be getting a little heated. He wondered if they were talking about the closed adoption and Dee's role in letting the truth come out. He'd defend the older woman, if Gabby ever spoke with him again.

It didn't look like today was going to be the day for that, though, judging from the troubled expression on Gabby's face.

And then Sloane came running directly from the slippy slide and threw her arms around Gabby.

"Excuse me," Noah said to Mr. Kennedy, and hustled toward Gabby and Sloane double-time. If he'd thought Gabby looked troubled before, now he'd label her expression as outright anguish.

He knew why, too. She was being hugged by a child she'd just learned was hers.

He had to intervene.

Chapter Six

"Something wrong, honey?" Gabby stroked Sloane's wet hair. Every cell in her body cried out *This is your child! Your child!*

Standing beside her, Dee tilted her head, watching, her eyes crinkled with sympathy.

And here came Noah. Dee's coconspirator. Gabby clenched her jaw against the angry words that wanted to come forth.

Sloane looked up at her. "Penelope says second grade is gonna be hard. I'm scared."

Just like that, Gabby's heart melted. "I get a little scared before school starts, too," she said, stunned and thankful that Sloane—her *daughter*—trusted Gabby enough to ask for reassurance.

"Where's Caramel?" Sloane asked.

"She's at home," Gabby said, "resting up, because she's coming to school with me tomorrow."

"She *is*?" Sloane sounded amazed.

"She is," Gabby said.

"I'm gonna tell Penelope!" Sloane yelled, and rushed off, leaving an imprint of her wet swimsuit down the front of Gabby's sundress.

"I'm sorry," Noah said.

"Are you, though?" Gabby lifted an eyebrow.

"I am. For…everything."

"As am I," Aunt Dee said.

Gabby blew out a breath. She loved Aunt Dee with all her heart, but the woman didn't know where her territory began and ended. Probably, it was the result of the dozen or more foster kids she'd helped raise. She'd often had to push hard at their boundaries in order to meet their needs and help them grow.

This time, though, her interfering was beyond the pale. She knew the situation with Todd, Gabby's ex, and yet she'd put Sloane at risk.

"I know you two have some talking to do," Aunt Dee said, apparently oblivious, "and I can be in on those conversations at some point. But not now." As if to prove her point, one of the neighbors rushed over to tell her that the condiments were running low.

"You two go talk," Dee directed. "Take a walk around the block. Get a few things figured out. You don't have to make any decisions today."

Only, they did, Gabby thought.

"Is that okay?" Noah asked her. "If it is, I'll let Sloane know where we're going and that we'll be close by." He waited for her answer, a humble expression on his face.

Sure. *Now* he was all humble.

"Fine," she said, and started toward the street.

He caught up with her a moment later. "Gabby, I am truly sorry. I hijacked your rights and I should have gone about this in an entirely different way. As soon as I thought through your reaction, I realized that."

She looked at him sideways. "You're a smart man," she said. "Why didn't you have the forethought to figure that out before you disrupted my life? And even worse, Sloane's life?"

He blew out a sigh. "After I made contact with Dee through the DNA service…well, it seemed like things came together so well. A birth mother with a great reputation, who loved kids. A beautiful, peaceful location. A caring relative on-site who could help us all deal with it."

"I'm furious at her, too, by the way," Gabby said.

"It's not her fault, it's mine," Noah said quickly. The shouts of the kids were distant now, the afternoon sun hot on Gabby's shoulders. "I'm the one who did the DNA search in the first place. She's too kind, that's all. I was at the end of my rope, and I ended up telling her about Sloane's mother's death and the way the whole thing affected Sloane."

"And she suggested you come here," Gabby said flatly.

"She did," Noah admitted. "She told us about the town and offered us a place to stay."

"And made us next-door neighbors." Gabby wasn't letting her aunt off the hook so easily. "I've known you and Sloane, what, a week? And I'm already totally enmeshed in your lives. I'm your neighbor, and I'm at least partly her teacher, and she's kind of…" Gabby's throat tightened. "She's kind of connected with me already. How am I supposed to respond to that kind of pressure?"

"If you say the word, we'll leave. Not leave the area, I can't disrupt her life that much again, but we'll move across town and I'll get her into the private elementary school."

"But I'm attached now, too!" Gabby kicked a stone, frustrated. "I can't just let it go, now that I know my daughter is right *there*. You have no idea how much I've longed for a child. No idea how completely awful it was to give away my beautiful, innocent baby. I wanted to raise her so much…" She trailed off, unable to say any more.

Noah walked alongside her as her steps slowed. "Hey. Why don't we sit down a minute?" They'd come to the small playground, surrounded by benches, at the edge of the cottage resort's common area. A couple of older kids were climbing the wooden structure, making warlike calls and chasing each other. Aside from them, the playground was deserted.

Numb, Gabby let Noah direct her to a bench. She accepted the handkerchief he gave her, and then laughed, tearfully. "You carry a *handkerchief*? In this day and age?"

"It's surprising how often it comes in handy," he said. And then he was blessedly silent.

Gabby wiped her eyes and blew her nose and took deep breaths. What was done was done. With Dee's encouragement and support, Noah had done this, and now she had no choice but to cope with it.

Fortunately, Gabby was good at coping. Her practical, resourceful side took over. "Look, I don't think it makes sense to tell Sloane about our connection yet. She's had a big change, coming here. School starts tomorrow, and that will be an adjustment. Adding the idea that her birth mother, who placed her for adoption, works at her school…that would be a lot."

"Excellent point," he said. "Let's see how the first week of school goes and then we'll regroup. Maybe even get a counselor involved with helping her understand and work through it."

"That makes sense. But Noah, we have to be so careful not to let other people get wind of this. My ex, Sloane's biological dad…he's very dangerous."

"Dangerous? How so?" Noah's voice was suddenly sharp.

"Abusive. Emotionally and physically. Vindictive. Cruel." As she said the words, Gabby felt like she was being melodramatic. But she was speaking the truth. Noah needed to know it.

"Where's he located?"

"I think he's still in Montana," she said, "but I'm not sure. I don't keep track of him, although maybe I should, now."

Noah propped his forearms on his thighs and clasped his hands, looking over at her. "I have some experience with bad players. I was a military cop. I can protect you and Sloane."

"You're not bulletproof." But it was true—Noah wouldn't be vulnerable to the kind of manipulation Todd was capable of. "Let's just keep this to ourselves for a little bit while we figure out our next steps."

He nodded agreement. But as they walked back, Gabby pressed her lips together and glanced sideways at him.

Like it or not, she was involved with him now. They were going to have to work together. There could be no more of those feelings of attraction she'd had when they'd spent that evening together. Now, everything had to stay businesslike, for Sloane's sake.

That might not be easy to do, but it was her only choice.

On Tuesday morning, Noah had two wishes: to get Sloane to her first day at school on a happy, or at least calm, note, and then to dig into his own backlogged work.

Sloane hadn't slept well. She'd cried out several times, frightened by some bad dream she couldn't remember. "Something about Mommy," she'd said, sniffling.

Finally, she'd fallen into a deeper sleep, and he had hopes that today might go okay. She'd put on her Penelope-approved outfit with excitement, a bright pink shirt and white cutoffs.

Through the open window, a fresh, slightly salty breeze cooled their cottage naturally. The sky was impossibly blue, with a couple of puffy marshmallow clouds floating around. Practically perfect for a first day of school. He imagined

Sloane running and playing and laughing with new friends at recess.

She'd eaten breakfast—peanut butter on whole wheat toast—and had even agreed to give her face a quick wipe with a washcloth and to brush her teeth.

Noah was watching out the window for Penelope and her mom, who'd kindly suggested they all walk to school together, when everything went south.

From the bathroom, he heard a familiar retching.

Uh-oh. He walked over and stood outside the door. "Honey, are you okay?"

"I'm sick," she said, her voice muffled. She retched again.

His own stomach plummeted, but he had a plan for this scenario, created with the help of a school counselor last year. "Wipe off your face when you're done," he said, keeping his voice calm and level. "You can choose what kind of mouthwash, bubble gum or grape. And then we'll head for school."

"I can't, Daddy."

"If you hurry, we can still walk with Penelope."

There was silence from the other side of the bathroom door. That, more than anything, told Noah that the retching was within Sloane's control.

He heard a tapping on the front door. It had to be Penelope. "Are you ready to go?" he asked Sloane.

"I can't!"

Noah went to the door, opened it, and told Penelope and her mom that they wouldn't be walking together today, but that Sloane would see Penelope later at school.

"Is she okay?" Penelope asked.

"She's fine," Noah assured them. "Just running a little late."

He waved to them and went back inside. From the bathroom, he heard the sound of water running and a few random banging noises. A moment later, Sloane came out, her face flushed, but relatively clean.

"Great job," he said, holding out his arms. Walking slowly, she came into them, and he hugged her close. Then he slid a hand to her forehead to check her temperature. No fever.

"Did Penelope leave?" She wiggled out of his arms.

He nodded. "They were worried they'd be late."

"*I'll* be late," she moaned.

"I'll drive you," he said quickly, before she could descend into a tantrum. "It'll be okay. We'll get there in plenty of time."

"It's not okay!" Her fists clenched.

He'd been in a fair number of challenging, combative situations in his previous career as a military cop. He couldn't remember anything that matched the battle of wills his own daughter was capable of implementing.

"Come on," he said. "Let's get your backpack and your lunch and get going."

"I feel sick again!" she cried. "I can't go!"

"You have to go," he told her gently.

"Mommy wouldn't make me!"

She was right, and that was the root of the problem. Sloane had gotten out of many days of kindergarten by feigning illness or throwing a tantrum. Someone had told him it took twice as long to uninstall a bad habit as it had taken to install it. By that math, he figured he was halfway there. They'd made it through first grade with decent attendance, although Noah had often found himself exhausted by the morning battle to get Sloane to school.

He'd hoped second grade would be an improvement, but he realized now the first day at a new school was bound to be rough. He'd been overly optimistic.

Wearily, he said, "If you're not at the front door by the count of three, you'll lose a privilege."

"That's not fair!" She planted her hands on her hips. "My consequences aren't on the board here. We don't even have a board."

Huh. He hadn't realized she had paid attention to the whiteboard back home, on which he'd listed behavioral consequences. She couldn't read them, of course, but he'd pointed to them sometimes, and she'd been through all of them many times. "One," he counted slowly. "Two. Th—"

"I'm going!" She ran through the living room and flung open the front door.

"Shoes," he said.

She looked wildly around, located her pink Crocs and slipped her feet into them, and ran out toward the SUV.

Noah grabbed her backpack and his keys and jogged after her.

Whew. They were going to make it.

He didn't envy Sloane's new teacher the task of caring for Sloane for the rest of the day. There was no help for it, though. The parent of a second grader couldn't stay in the classroom.

Gabby had said she was doing her special reading program with Caramel today. Would Sloane be invited to participate? And how would that go? How would it make Gabby feel?

If he'd pitied himself for his own difficult morning, he should pity her more.

He dropped Sloane off when his turn came in the car line, grateful there was a teacher there to greet her and guide her to the right place, grateful it wasn't Gabby.

And then he drove home to try to focus on the book he was writing, rather than imagining how Sloane—and Gabby— were managing their first day of school.

* * *

An hour after the students had left, Gabby drove home in a first-day daze. Returning to school was a challenge for young kids, and she always expected to have to review rules and make corrections and practice lots of patience.

This day, though, had been more complicated than usual for two reasons: Caramel and Sloane.

Bringing Caramel on the first day hadn't been the wisest decision. She'd wanted to start as she meant to go on, and she and Caramel would do reading sessions a couple of days each week.

The little Yorkie had done well, resting in her crate for part of the morning and afternoon, and coming out for circle time and a reading demonstration. The kids had been thrilled. Still, her presence had contributed to the chaos of the day, making some of the kids wild with excitement.

When Sloane had attended one of Gabby's small-group, introductory reading sessions...wow.

It wasn't that Sloane's behavior had been bad in Gabby's session. The poor child had looked exhausted, but she'd visibly exhaled when she'd come into the room and seen Gabby and Caramel. She'd flopped down into the chair Gabby had pointed to and propped her chin on her hands and listened quietly.

The intense thing had been Gabby's own reaction. Every time she looked at the little girl, she felt a bigger and bigger tug of emotions. This child was her daughter. Gabby might actually have the chance to get to know her, even help raise her—or at least be an adult influence. The thought of that brought a deep sense of joy, even awe.

At the same time, Gabby had seen that Sloane acted out in the hallway, and she'd heard in the break room that Sloane's teacher was struggling to manage her.

And this wasn't just an interesting new kid acting out at school. It was *her* kid. She was embarrassed and worried and stressed out about Sloane's misbehavior. On some level, she felt like it was her fault. Like she had to fix it.

She pulled into the gravel driveway at the side of her cottage. Beside her, Caramel was asleep in her crate, and Gabby was half tempted to lean her head back and take a nap herself.

But a glance at her tote bag, already bristling with paperwork, made her groan and climb out of the car. She gathered her purse, her tote and an inspirational poster that had somehow gotten ripped over the summer and needed repair. She was tugging Caramel's crate out of the passenger's side when she felt someone lifting her bags out of her hands.

She turned. Noah.

"Hand me Caramel," he said, holding out a free hand.

She hooked the crate on his fingers. "Thanks," she said, and led the way to her cottage. She unlocked the door, then took things one at a time from his arms and set them inside. She released Caramel from her crate so the little dog could run around the yard. Then she sat wearily on her front steps.

"Mind if I join you for just a minute?" Noah asked.

"No, as long as you don't have a second grader in tow," she said. Then she clapped a hand over her mouth. "Did I really say that? I love the kids. I just need a little time off, that's all."

"Understandable. Sloane's at Penelope's for another hour, so I think we're safe. How was your day?"

"Honestly, it was a little rough. If you're asking about Sloane, she wasn't a behavior problem in my class, although she refused to join the reading circle. I saw her get into a pretty loud argument in the hall, though. Word in the teachers' lounge is that she earned a spot in the time-out corner twice."

Noah sighed. "I can't say I'm surprised."

"She wasn't the only kid acting out. The first day is always a challenge with young kids."

"Thanks for letting me know. And for softening it. I heard from Penelope that Sloane said mean things to a couple of other kids."

"I'm sure she wasn't the only one, but…it's something to work on." Caramel ran over and put her paws up on Gabby's knee, and she pulled the little dog into her lap. "Caramel was a distraction. I probably shouldn't have brought her on the first day, but live and learn."

"That's my parental motto," Noah said. "I will definitely work with Sloane on manners and school behavior. If you have any suggestions, I would welcome them."

"I'll try to come up with some ideas," Gabby said.

Noah was asking questions as Sloane's parent. Clearly, he took responsibility for her actions, which was admirable.

But Gabby was her parent, too, and she felt the responsibility of that pushing down on her. After all, she'd placed Sloane for adoption. Maybe Sloane acted out because of some sense of being abandoned. "Sloane knows she's adopted, right?"

Noah nodded. "That's what most professionals advise. It works better for kids to know their history from a young age. Of course, you adjust the details according to the child's developmental stage."

"Does she ask about it?"

He hesitated. "She does," he said slowly. "Especially since her mom passed away."

"And what do you say?" Gabby suddenly felt breathless.

"I tell her that her parents knew they couldn't take care of her, so they wanted to find a family who could," he said. "And that was us. Since Bridgette died, though, she's asked a couple of times whether her birth mother might want her back."

"Oh, wow." Gabby let her head sink into her hands.

"Of course, I reassure her that I'm never letting her go. Look, we can talk about all of this, but you have to be beat from the first day of school. Why don't you go take a nap, then come and have dinner with us? I'm grilling burgers, nothing fancy. But at least that way you won't have to cook."

Gabby *was* a little hungry. She hadn't had time for lunch today. And the thought of pulling a meal together had no appeal. At the same time, she was concerned and upset and confused over her new knowledge about Sloane.

Noah must have read the ambivalence on her face. "If you're not up to company, that's fine. I'll just bring you a plate of food. It's the least I can do, since you put up with my ornery kid for at least part of the day."

"Your ornery kid who's also *my* ornery kid." But she was too weary to argue. "You definitely got the nap idea right. I may come over, but if I'm too tired, I'll text to let you know."

"Of course." He stood with graceful ease, and she was suddenly oddly conscious of how well he moved.

She rubbed her temples and watched him walk across the yard to his cottage. Yeah, she was officially losing it if she was enjoying the sight of a man who'd turned her life upside down.

Two hours later, Gabby woke up to the sound of a tap at her door. She checked the clock, sat up and groaned.

Despite Noah's suggestion that she take a nap, she hadn't intended to conk out. But a few minutes on the couch had turned into a full-scale deep sleep. She ran her hands through her hair and went to the door.

It was Aunt Dee. "Good morning, sunshine!" she joked.

"Noah sent me over to see whether you wanted to join us for dinner. He invited Mr. Kennedy, too. If you don't want to come, I'm to come back with a plate of food."

"You and Noah sure seem to be good buddies," Gabby said, feeling grumpy.

"He's a good man in a difficult situation," her aunt responded. "Come to dinner. I brought mac and cheese, and he's grilling."

Gabby could smell burgers on the grill, and her stomach growled. "It's tempting," she said, "but I don't know if I can be all sweet and social. I'm still mad at what the two of you did."

"Understood," her aunt said. "Can I come in while you think about it?"

"Sure." Gabby held the door open. Aunt Dee came in, and while Gabby changed clothes and washed her face, Aunt Dee kept up a running conversation from the living room. "How are you handling all of this?" she asked.

"It's awful," Gabby said. "I can't believe my daughter, whom I just met a week ago, has a conduct disorder that's probably my fault."

"What?" Aunt Dee called through the bedroom door. "Why would you think that's your fault?"

"I placed her for adoption. She knows her mother gave her up. That's got to have an impact."

"Honey." Aunt Dee came into the room as Gabby ran a brush over her hair. "You know very well that there are plenty of well-adjusted adopted kids," she said. "I was adopted, and I'm one of the better adjusted people I know." She guffawed at her own joke.

"Well, Sloane *isn't* well adjusted. Of course I blame myself."

Her aunt frowned. "Remember, there's some genetics involved. Your husband was volatile. Maybe some of that came down to Sloane, or maybe it's nurture, or a lack thereof. Probably a little of both. But you did the best you could at the time. Sloane's safe, and healthy, and has a great dad."

"She does," Gabby said. She flopped back down on her bed, suddenly exhausted again. "You know what? I think I'm going to pass on the lovely family dinner. I'll heat up something."

"Don't do that," her aunt said. "I'll bring over a plate of food. You take it easy." She was treating Gabby like she was made of glass, and it felt strange.

Stranger still, to eat a delicious grilled meal quietly at her own house, while next door Sloane, Noah, Aunt Dee and Mr. Kennedy shared a meal complete with laughter and music Gabby could faintly hear.

This was just…sad.

Was this how she wanted to live? To be on the outside of a family? To turn down invitations and grow old alone? Like cranky Mr. Kennedy?

Quit being dramatic, she told herself. *Also, Mr. Kennedy is socializing. You're the one who's turning down invitations and staying home.*

She thought of the chocolate chip cookies she'd made for church and had left behind. She'd meant to take them to school, put them out in the teachers' lounge, but she'd forgotten.

She stood up. Now was a time to share them, before they got stale. She pulled out the big Tupperware container of cookies, ran a comb through her hair, and washed the plate on which Aunt Dee had brought her dinner. Then she snapped a leash on Caramel and headed across the lawn to Noah's cottage.

Chapter Seven

As Gabby approached Noah's front door, she heard a deep voice followed by Sloane's high-pitched one. Some kind of argument. She slowed down.

"Stop right there, child." The deep voice didn't belong to Noah, but to Mr. Kennedy. "Does your father know you're leaving the house?"

Gabby could barely make out the older man standing in front of the stoop blocking Sloane's exit. Uh-oh. Two volatile people. She stopped in the shadow of a couple of tall bushes, ready to intervene if needed.

"What's it to you?" Sloane snapped.

Uh-oh. Gabby braced herself for the explosion. Mr. Kennedy was big on respect.

But to her surprise, the older man didn't lay into her. "Why were you sneaking out?" he asked.

"I wanted to go see Caramel. Don't tell Daddy."

"Humph. Sit down." It wasn't a request. It was an order. Mr. Kennedy gestured toward the steps.

Gabby couldn't see Sloane's expression, but she could guess it. The kid had to be ready to blow after a long day of trying to follow orders in school.

Gabby picked up Caramel and stroked her to keep her calm in the face of what was likely to be a loud fight.

To Gabby's surprise, Sloane sat down. To her even greater surprise, Mr. Kennedy carefully lowered himself onto the steps beside her.

Around them, the sound of crickets rose in a loud chorus, then fell. The air was cool and fresh.

"What happens when you do things you're not supposed to do?" Mr. Kennedy asked.

"I get a time-out," Sloane said, looking up at him.

"And your dad gets upset. Scared."

"Don't tell him!" Sloane snapped, standing up, hands on hips. "I. Want. To. See. Caramel!"

Here it came. Before Gabby could react, Mr. Kennedy raised one hand like a stop sign. "Quit that right now," he said, his voice low and stern. "If you're going to yell, we're done talking."

Sloane stood still for a minute. The explosion Gabby expected didn't materialize.

"Sit back down," Mr. Kennedy ordered.

Sloane hesitated, then did as she was told.

Gabby's mouth fell open. She petted Caramel gently, keeping her quiet.

"Thank you. Now. Why did you want to see that little dog so much?"

There was a moment of silence. Then, in a low voice, Sloane said, "'Cause she'll teach me to read."

Mr. Kennedy shook his head. Gabby could practically hear his eyes rolling. "A dog can't teach you to read," he said. "For that, you have to pay attention in school."

Great, undermine what I'm trying to do with the Read to Dogs program.

"I don't like school," Sloane said, a little whine in her voice.

"That doesn't matter. You won't like everything you have to do."

"But I don't…" Sloane trailed off.

"If you want something, you have to work hard to get it. It might not be fun."

Sloane was quiet for a moment. Then she spoke. "I wanna have fun."

"Uh-huh." Mr. Kennedy was quiet for a minute. "Everybody wants to have fun. But nobody gets what they want all the time. Nobody has fun all the time."

Way to depress a kid, Gabby thought. Now, surely, Sloane would blow up.

Gabby heard voices rising from the screened-in porch from the back of the house. Quickly, she set down her cookies, shifted Caramel, and texted Noah. He needed to know where Sloane was, so he didn't worry and could intervene if necessary. Sloane on front steps talking with Mr. Kennedy. And probably about to flip out on him.

But she didn't. She just looked up at the older man.

"Learning to read might not be fun like playing with a dog," he lectured. "It might mean sitting still when you feel like running around."

Sloane slumped and looked away.

"Can I tell you a secret?" Mr. Kennedy asked.

"Okay."

"I hated school."

Behind the pair, the front door of the cottage opened a crack. Gabby could see from the height of the figure inside that it was Noah. But he didn't come out. Neither Sloane nor Mr. Kennedy seemed to notice him.

Sloane shuffled her feet. "You went to school?" she asked Mr. Kennedy. "But you're so old."

The older man made a sound like a snort. "Believe it or

not, I went to school. Quite a lot of it. Sat there bored out of my mind. I wanted to be outside."

"Me, too." Sloane scooted a little closer to Mr. Kennedy. "Did you sneak out?"

"No, because I'd get a whipping if I did."

Sloane nodded. "My mommy hit me sometimes," she said matter-of-factly.

Gabby's breath went out of her in a big sigh. Did Noah know? If he hadn't before, he did now.

Mr. Kennedy was quiet.

"But," Sloane said, "Mommy went up." She pointed at the sky. "And Daddy doesn't hit me."

Mr. Kennedy cleared his throat. "Your dad knows best. You know what?"

"What?"

"I'm glad I went to school, even though I had a hard time sitting still through it."

"You are?"

A little light came through the door. Noah must have opened it wider. But the pair on the steps still didn't seem to notice.

"I'm glad I went to school, because I got to become a zoologist. Do you know what that is?"

Sloane, now more visible in the light from the door behind her, shook her head.

"After a whole lot of schooling, I got to have a job with animals. I loved that job." His voice was wistful. "I was happy every day doing it, and all because of school."

Gabby's throat tightened a little. She hadn't known Mr. Kennedy had had a big career, one he'd loved. The cranky old man took on another dimension in her mind.

"Now," he said, "you'd better go back inside before your dad worries about you."

"Okay," Sloane said. Either she was more agreeable and relaxed, or she was tired from her day.

Mr. Kennedy stood up stiffly, one hand going to his lower back. "If you come to see me sometime, I'll show you my hamster," he said.

"You have a *hamster*?" Sloane sounded amazed. "What's its name?"

"Atticus. I have a book about hamsters, too. We can sit on the porch and bring the hamster out with us and look at the book together."

"Okay!" Sloane stood, bouncing on her toes.

Mr. Kennedy raised a hand. "But only if your dad says okay, and if you're nice and quiet. No yelling. I don't like a lot of noise."

"Okay!"

As Mr. Kennedy walked off, his gait slow, Gabby could just make out a little smile on his face.

Sloane started to run inside and crashed into her father. "Daddy! Guess what!" They walked inside together, Sloane telling him about Atticus, the hamster she was going to meet.

Noah said something to Sloane, then came back and held open the door. "You out here, Gabby?" he called.

"Yes." She picked up her cookies, walked toward him, and climbed the steps. "That was sweet."

"Thanks for the heads-up," he said, stepping aside so she could enter the cottage.

As she eased by him, she felt his warmth and had the absurd inclination to touch him, hug him, somehow get closer.

Apparently, parenting a child together made you feel mushy and emotional. In her situation, though, that was ridiculous. Maybe she *shouldn't* have come, but she was committed now.

Sloane's eyes got round when she saw Gabby, the big

container of cookies and Caramel. "Can I have a cookie and walk your dog?" she asked breathlessly.

"You can have a cookie if it's okay with your dad." Gabby handed the container to Noah. "It's getting dark for a walk, but you may play with Caramel if you're gentle."

"I will be! Can she watch my show with me?"

Gabby looked at Noah and shrugged. "Okay with me."

"One show," he said to Sloane, "and then you'll bring Caramel back and get ready for bed."

"Okay!" Sloane took the leash from Gabby and walked the little dog into the cottage's living room.

"We can keep an eye on things from here on the back porch," Noah said. "I'm glad you came. Sit down, and I'll get you some lemonade."

Aunt Dee moved her chair to make room for Gabby to sit down and squeezed her hand. "I'm glad you came over, too. And not just because of the cookies." She took one, bit into it, smiled, and nodded. "But. You're an excellent baker. These are superb."

Noah brought her lemonade out and sat down at the table. He took a cookie, too. For a few minutes, the three of them sat quietly, munching and sipping while the sound of crickets rose and fell outside.

Gabby hated to break the pleasant mood, but she felt she should speak up about what Sloane had said. "Were you aware your wife hit Sloane?"

Aunt Dee gasped.

Gabby explained the context and what Sloane had said.

"I was." Noah sighed. "I found out when I saw her smack Sloane one Saturday. Sloane wasn't hurt, physically, but I could tell it wasn't the first time. I didn't like that way of parenting and I told my wife so. She promised not to do it again, but she also withdrew more from Sloane after that."

Gabby let out a breath. Not good.

Finally, Dee spoke. "What's past is past. I'm glad you're both here." She paused, then added, "It's what I envisioned when I talked Noah into moving down here. All three of us caring about and loving on that little girl. Loving her right back to where she needs to be, happy and carefree."

Her aunt's vision was idyllic. Too idyllic. "Happy and carefree for now," Gabby said. "What happens if Todd finds out we're all here together?"

"If he hasn't come after you yet, dear, do you really think he's going to? Especially when he's—" Aunt Dee waved an arm toward the outdoors "—when he's all the way out in Montana?"

Gabby knew Aunt Dee was probably right, but she couldn't shake her unease. "I'm just afraid," Gabby said. "He's shrewd. He probably does know where I'm located or could figure it out if he were motivated. If he saw a photo, say, of me and Sloane together, he'd know she was his child, and then…"

"I stay away from social media," Noah said. "And can't we put her on some kind of 'do not photograph' list at the school?"

"Yes. You should have gotten a form about that. Make sure you turn it in."

"I will. And since Sloane has a different last name, even if a friend's parent did post a picture, how would he recognize her?"

"If she were with Gabby, he might," Aunt Dee said. "They do look alike."

"I guess that's true," Gabby said. "Let's all stay aware, okay?"

"Of course," Noah said. "Even in peaceful times, you should always be prepared for battle."

Their talk moved on to other things. Pretty soon Sloane's show was over, and she brought Caramel back without prompting, which was a pleasant surprise. It was good to know Sloane didn't always exhibit her ODD. Maybe hers was a mild case.

But any child did better with consistency and sleep, and it was Sloane's bedtime. As Gabby and her aunt left, Gabby reflected that now, talking about Sloane with her aunt and Noah, she was more than ever enmeshed in the little family's life. She needed to be careful, not just of exterior dangers like her ex, but of her heart.

Chapter Eight

"We did it!" Another teacher high-fived Gabby as they made their way to the end-of-day activity period, conducted outside on Fridays when the weather was fair.

"One week down," Gabby agreed as she led her second graders outside.

The first week of school was always a little chaotic, but Gabby felt good about how her class, as well as the reading program, was starting out. Now, she'd get to recruit a few more kids to participate in the latter.

In the fenced-in field that adjoined the playground, various tables were set up, as well as some stations for soccer and running games. Teachers and staff members stood by the tables, welcoming students and demonstrating activities.

"You may look at any of the tables on this side of the field," she said to her students. "Choose two clubs or activities you like, and that will be your Friday Fun Activity for the first part of the year. If your parents come to pick you up, or your bus is called, check in with your teacher before you leave." She asked them to repeat the instructions back to her and then turned them loose. She picked up Caramel's carrier and headed to the library table.

"You're giving us an unfair advantage," the school librarian said, laughing as Gabby set up a small pen for Caramel.

She added a little cushion—Caramel was a bit of a princess, and didn't always like to lie directly on the grass—and then got the little dog out of the sling she'd been carrying her in.

The librarian's words proved true: a crowd of students quickly gathered around them. "Reading to dogs is only part of the library club," she reminded the kids. "You'll be able to choose extra books to take home, and...they're writing stories too, aren't they, Maria?"

"Yes, and we're going to have a blast!" Maria was new to the school and full of enthusiasm. She greeted each child and asked them about their favorite picture books. She'd brought stuffed animals and toys to go with various books, and there was a table with art supplies for recreating book covers and drawing pictures of characters.

Gabby chose Caleb, one of her students who'd struggled with reading last year, to demonstrate how to read to Caramel. A small circle of kids settled around to watch and offer commentary. Caramel sat alert, her ears perked up, seeming to listen.

It was a cute scene, and Gabby snapped several photos to include in her application for another year of grant funding.

Gabby passed out numbers, like those in a supermarket deli, so that the kids would know whose turn it was and could proceed in an organized way. The students behaved well—a relief, since parents would be arriving soon. Gabby wanted the parents to understand what a good program Read to Dogs was, and the risk was always that the kids would get too excited and chaos would ensue.

So far, so good. When her demonstration reader was finished, Gabby chose another child from the audience to read to Caramel, keeping the selection brief so as many kids as possible could participate.

When Sloane's turn came, she refused to read, but she

stayed in the group, listening. That was okay. She was learning by listening and watching.

"It's great to see kids clamoring to read," Maria said.

"Especially mine," a newly arrived mother said. More parents gathered, and Gabby had the opportunity to explain the program to them.

When Noah joined the group, Gabby felt all her senses sharpen. It had to be just because of the Sloane connection, didn't it?

But the warm awareness that suffused her face and chest told another tale. He was the best-looking dad here, and probably the most professionally successful and well-known, too. Of course Gabby felt a little spark. She was fairly certain that most of the other single women here did, too.

She fanned her face and went over to chat with him, warning herself to keep things friendly and professional. Just because they were neighbors, just because they had a strong connection through Sloane, didn't mean she should act as if they were best friends.

"You're the most popular club here," Noah said.

"I credit Caramel," Gabby said. "And Maria, the new librarian. Between them, Sloane's bound to get into books and reading. Any kid would."

They both watched Sloane, who sat listening intently as each child read a little to Caramel.

"How's your work going?" she asked.

"Well, I think," he said. "I took your advice and visited that nautical history museum. It's going to enrich the storyline of my novel."

"That's great!" Gabby felt a little glow. "When your book comes out, I'll be able to say I had an influence."

"Your name will be on the acknowledgements page," he said, smiling at her.

Her breath caught a little at the sparkle in his eyes.

Suddenly, there was a low, quiet growl. Caramel's growl. Gabby spun around.

"She bit me!" yelled Bradley Bowen, a superactive kid who'd barely passed Gabby's class last year. He was jumping around, holding a hand over his opposite forearm.

Gabby rushed over. "What happened?" she asked, kneeling beside Bradley and touching his shoulder in an effort to get him to stay still. He was glaring at Caramel, who'd retreated to the back of her pen, the hair on her back standing high.

"Let me see your arm, Bradley," Gabby said when the child had stopped jumping. She reached for his arm. "I need to know what happened."

"No!" Bradley pulled his arm away.

Bradley's mother approached, and Gabby groaned inwardly. The woman was almost as high-strung as her son.

Bradley stood and buried his face in his mother's side. "That dog bit me," he mumbled.

The mother straightened, her brow wrinkling. "This is completely unacceptable. Why would you have an out-of-control dog at a children's school event?"

Caramel was cowering in the back of the pen, and Gabby picked her up and nestled her into her sling. She was quivering, but when Bradley pulled away from his mother and started jumping around, coming closer, Caramel let out another growl and bared her tiny teeth.

A small crowd had gathered, which wasn't forwarding Gabby's goal of making this program appealing, but the main thing was making sure a child hadn't been hurt. "Let us see your arm, Bradley," she said, "or we'll call the nurse and she can check it, if you'd rather."

His lower lip sticking out, Bradley uncovered the place he'd been holding on his arm.

Gabby looked at the unmarked skin, and relief flooded her. "I don't see any wound. Exactly what happened, Bradley?" she asked.

"Your dog bit me," he insisted.

"That would be a first," she said, "but let's have the nurse come look at your arm just to make sure you're okay." She sent one of her reliable students to get the school nurse.

"If a dog bit you," another boy said, "you might have to get rabies shots!"

Bradley's eyes widened.

"Not to mention the likelihood of a lawsuit," Bradley's mother said in a snotty tone.

Suddenly, Sloane was in front of Bradley, his mom and Gabby, hands on hips. "Caramel didn't bite you," she said, her voice loud and clear. "You put your hand in the pen and grabbed her by the collar and tried to pull her out! You were hurting her and she just growled at you!"

"Fact," another boy said.

Several other kids nodded.

"Shut up!" Bradley yelled in Sloane's face. "You're a liar!"

"Am not!" Sloane yelled back.

Gabby stepped between the two children as Sloane drew back her fist. Bradley's mother sputtered ineffectually. Fortunately, the school nurse appeared, assessed the situation instantly, and led Bradley away, beckoning for his mother to follow. Noah, meanwhile, reached Sloane and knelt in front of her. "Deep breaths," he said in his low, calming rumble of a voice. "You did a good job telling everyone what really happened."

"You did, honey," Gabby said. "Thank you for that. Caramel and I both appreciate it."

Sloane's upraised arm dropped to her side, and she looked from her father to Gabby and back again, as if she couldn't believe what she was hearing.

"Can I still read to Caramel?" a little girl asked. Marnie was a sweet, quiet child who'd been waiting patiently since the line had formed.

Gabby made a snap decision: it was better to end on a high note. "Yes, but you'll be the last one to read to her today," she said. "And I'll hold her while you read." She sat down, patted a spot beside her, and waited while the child read a short picture book to the dog.

She took Noah's advice to Sloane and sucked in some deep breaths herself. She loved the Read to Dogs program, but dogs were animals. Caramel was an animal. Well trained, but if threatened, she'd react.

Allowing calm little Marnie Anderson to read to Caramel was the right decision. The little dog settled down and stopped shaking, and Gabby calmed down, too. When other parents came and picked their kids up, several remarked on the sweet sight. Buses were being called, and kids were checking in with teachers and then leaving for the day.

Gabby smiled and encouraged the last little reader, but inside, turmoil churned.

If she'd been paying closer attention, she could have stopped Bradley's rough behavior before it turned into a real problem. She should never have let herself be distracted by Noah.

It was just one more reason she should pay attention to her teaching job and not to men. When her marriage had ended, she'd decided to concentrate on something she could control—her work—rather than taking another chance on a relationship. Now, she was letting a friendly, kind guy like Noah pose too much of a distraction and put her job at risk. She had to refocus.

When all the kids had been picked up, Gabby helped put away tables and supplies and then made her way to the car. She could have kicked herself for looking around for Noah's SUV and then being disappointed that Noah had gone on home.

She had to get a grip on herself and her out-of-control emotions.

Chapter Nine

On Saturday, an old-fashioned truck squealed into Noah's driveway, the horn making a distinctive *ah-OOO-ga* sound.

"Who wants to go to the sunflower farm?" Dee called from the open window.

Noah was at his computer, trying to get a little writing done while Sloane watched Saturday morning TV. In a second, she was running outside, still in her pajamas.

"Sloane! Wait! Remember the rules!"

Sloane knew she wasn't allowed to go outside without checking with Noah, but he'd relaxed that dictum a little here in Chesapeake Corners. It was so much safer here, but Noah was conscious of Gabby's concerns about her ex. And kids were at least somewhat at risk, no matter what kind of town they lived in.

Sloane ran back in. "It's Miss Dee, and she wants us to go to some farm with her! She says it's real pretty. Can we?"

"Let me talk to her." Noah saved his document and rubbed a hand over his face. He'd made progress on his book idea last night after Sloane had gone to bed, and he was eager to keep moving with it. On the other hand, it was a sunny Saturday, and he couldn't expect Sloane to sit quietly in front of the TV all day.

He went outside just as Gabby came out, Caramel on a leash beside her, and Noah's breath caught.

She wore jeans and a red shirt, her hair loose around her shoulders, and she looked…well, she looked gorgeous, even more than usual. She waved to him and then leaned on the open passenger's side window, talking to her aunt. Both of them smiled as he approached.

He took a couple of deep breaths, trying to quell his odd reaction to Gabby's appearance.

"I don't know if you meant to invite us, too," he said, staying on the driver's side, "but Sloane took it that way."

"Oh, I want you all to come," Dee said. "My friend who runs the farm told me the zinnias and sunflowers are at their peak. It'll be gorgeous out there."

"I'm in," Gabby said promptly. "Flowers are my thing. I love them."

Sloane started jumping up and down. "Will you bring Caramel, too?"

Gabby tilted her head to one side. "She'd love to go, but I don't want to wear her out. Tell you what, I'll drive myself, and that way I can bring Caramel home when she gets tired."

"Can I ride with you?" Sloane asked.

There was an awkward silence. Gazes flickered between Noah, Dee and Gabby. They all knew what Sloane didn't: that Gabby was her birth mother.

They needed to decide when and how to tell Sloane, Noah realized, provided Gabby was in full agreement about letting her know the truth. He hadn't actually asked her, or if he had, he hadn't gotten an answer.

"There's a petting zoo and hayrides and an art show," Dee said. "Something for everyone. If you want to drive separately, that's fine."

"But can I ride with you, Miss Gabby?"

Sloane's voice rose to a whine.

"Give Miss Gabby a minute to decide. You need to go get dressed and wash your face, anyway."

She opened her mouth to protest.

Noah raised his eyebrows and shook his head.

"Okay! I'll go wash up!" Sloane ran inside, and Noah stayed behind.

"Totally up to you," he said to Gabby. "You won't get a moment of silence if she rides with you." He was trying to keep it light, but he could see from Gabby's face that the opportunity to drive Sloane somewhere, by herself, was a little fraught. Of course it was. She was still getting used to the idea that Sloane was her daughter.

As for Sloane, she had no idea.

"It's fine if she rides with me and Caramel," Gabby said finally, and smiled with her usual positive attitude. "Just let me run inside and get dressed and get Caramel ready. Ten minutes." She disappeared into the house.

"And you'll ride with me," Dee said, "and we'll talk."

Twenty minutes later, they were on the road, driving through the farm territory of the Eastern Shore, Noah and Dee in Dee's truck, Gabby behind them with Sloane and Caramel. "Everyone thinks of the water when they think of the Eastern Shore," Dee said, "but our main industry is actually farming. Corn, wheat, barley, rye…you name it, we grow it."

Noah spotted a couple of tiny deer by the side of the road. "What are those?" he asked. He held an arm out the window to point to them, hoping that Gabby and Sloane would see the delicate creatures.

"Sika deer," Dee said. "They have an exotic background. Brought all the way from Japan way back in the early 1900s. Pretty, aren't they?"

"They are." Noah leaned back, farm-fresh air blowing

over him, sun warming his arm on the open window. "It's an interesting area."

"Glad you came?" Dee asked, steering around a bend.

"In a lot of ways, yes," he said. "It's relaxing here, and rich with history. That's good for my work. What's more important, it seems to agree with Sloane. She's a little calmer, and she's making some friends." She'd played with other kids two days after school this week, once with Penelope, and once with a tourist family in the cottage resort. "It's great for her to be able to get outside more, to run and be active. I hadn't really thought about the benefits that would have for her, but I think it's going to help."

"Fresh air and exercise," Dee said. "Those lead to good appetite and good sleep. That's at least half of what kids need, I always thought."

Noah nodded. Dee had the parenting experience to know what she was talking about.

"How do you feel it's working out with Gabby?" Dee asked.

Noah looked out the window. "She's a great person," he said. "I can see how good she is, or could be, for Sloane. But I didn't think this through. I'm completely disrupting her life, and she didn't ask for that."

"She didn't," Dee said thoughtfully. "But sometimes, a disruption of plans can be a good thing. A blessing. With God's help, this could work out really well. You could be parents to Sloane together."

"That's true," he said, and the thought made him as excited as a kid on Christmas morning. Which was *not* the right way for a responsible person, a father, to feel. He ought to be calm and measured, weighing out whether this plan was the best for all involved.

But it had been so long since he'd had someone with whom

to share his feelings about parenthood. Someone with whom he could discuss Sloane's issues. Someone who cared about her as much as he did.

His wife hadn't been that person, unfortunately. But Gabby, who'd only known for a week that she was Sloane's mom, already seemed to care for her, and more deeply than he had any right to expect.

"This is a phase," Dee said. "If the two of you decide to co-parent, it will be good for all of you, I think. Gabby will have the child she's been wanting, the child she's mourned all these years. Sloane will have a mom. And you'll have help. Once that's all established, you can move away so you're not next door and in each other's pockets all the time. Sloane will get older and won't be in Gabby's path professionally as much. I think it'll be good for all concerned."

"You're right," Noah said slowly. The thought of moving beyond this phase, of not being near Gabby, of having Sloane grow older and spread her wings…all of it was a little disturbing to him.

"You'll figure it out," Dee said with confidence as she turned down a dirt road. A sign read Meekers' Sunflower Farm. They parked, and behind them, Gabby and Sloane got out of the car. "See what I mean?" Dee said, nodding toward them. "Mother and daughter. People will start to notice, so it'll be better if Sloane's on board."

"I'm not completely sure Gabby is on board," Noah responded, watching Gabby and Sloane hover over Caramel, laughing together, their blond heads close. Something about the sight made his throat get tight.

"You need an opportunity to talk about it," Dee said. "Maybe you'll get the chance today."

Noah looked around at the beautiful fields of sunflowers on one side of the road, stretching golden into the horizon, and several smaller fields of multicolored zinnias on the other. "Wow," he said. "If I'm going to have an important conversation with the mother of my child, this is a great place to do it."

"You're welcome," Dee said with a knowing smile. And suddenly, Noah wondered if she'd set up the whole thing for that very purpose.

Even if she had, Noah couldn't find it in his heart to object. He was looking forward to this day with his daughter and Gabby.

Gabby loved wandering Meekers' Sunflower Farm with Aunt Dee and Noah and Sloane. Caramel alternated between trotting alongside them on a leash, enjoying the attention of dog-loving farm visitors, and riding in Gabby's sling, from whence she barked boldly at the few other, much larger dogs who were there with their families.

Sloane's eyes widened as she took in the fields of flowers. She smiled when she tasted the fresh peaches and apples for sale in the farm's quaint shop. When she realized she could ride in a little train that wove through the zinnia fields, she literally jumped for joy.

"You're a farm girl at heart, aren't you, honey?" Aunt Dee asked her when she climbed off the train and ran to tell them about it.

"Yes!" Sloane looked up at her father. "I'm a farm girl! Can we live on a farm, Daddy?"

He laughed. He'd been doing a lot of that today, and it was good to see. "I wouldn't be a very good farmer, muffin," he said, "but it's nice to live where we can visit farms, isn't it?"

"Yeah!" Then Sloane leaned against him and yawned, enormously.

Gabby and her aunt were already sitting on benches outside the farm's little shop, and now Noah joined them, pulling Sloane into his lap.

Gabby looked down at Caramel, who had fallen asleep in her sling. "Might be time for us to go," she said. "Caramel's beat."

"Tell you what," Dee said. "I'm ready to leave, too. Why don't I take Caramel and Sloane, and head back to the cottages? The two of you can stay and see what the place is like at sunset." She winked at Gabby.

Gabby's face heated. What was Aunt Dee implying?

Noah looked from her to Aunt Dee and back again. He'd obviously seen their interaction. She wondered what he thought of it.

"Sloane," he said, "could you take this tip to the train driver, please?" He held out a five-dollar bill.

It was a mark of how tired she was that she didn't argue. She just obediently took the money over to the man who'd driven the train.

"We do have some things to discuss," he said to Gabby once Sloane was out of earshot. "I'd like to do that sooner rather than later. What do you think, Gabby? Do you mind staying behind so we can talk?"

She leaned back in her chair. What did she think?

She thought it would be fun to hang out here at the farm with just Noah. A lot of fun. Maybe dangerously fun, because he was a charming, attractive man and she'd been noticing that a lot today.

Also, she knew that he wanted to talk about what to do about Sloane, and she didn't have an answer, not for sure.

But would she ever? And would it ever be easy to talk to Noah? "It's as good a time as any," she said finally. "If we can get Sloane to agree."

But Aunt Dee, with her years of experience wrangling

children, had the solution. "Sloane," she said, "I'm tired and I want to go home. Caramel's tired, too. I'd like to take her, but only if she has someone to sit in the back seat beside her. How would you feel about riding along with me and helping me take care of her?"

"I can do it!" Sloane said. Then she looked at her father. "Can I, Daddy?"

He frowned, as if he had to think it over. "Yes," he said finally, "if you do what Miss Dee says, and help with Caramel. I can give you money to stop for dinner," he added to Dee.

She waved a hand. "Why would we do that," she said, "when I have the fixings for walking tacos at home? And I'd like to make brownies for dessert, but that's a lot of work. I would need someone to help with that."

"I'll help!" Sloane cried out.

And so it was done, and Gabby and Noah were soon waving to Aunt Dee and Sloane as they headed off in her truck.

She looked over at him, and something tightened inside her. She'd told herself from the moment that she'd met him that he wasn't a typically handsome man, and that was still true. But he looked…intelligent. Thoughtful. And then there were those muscular arms, and the fact that he towered over her, making her feel petite… She swallowed and tried to bring her thoughts back to where they should be.

She should be focused on the serious business they had to deal with, not on his looks and his very masculine presence. A better person would focus only on his—their—daughter, and what was best for her. And Gabby *was* focused on that, mostly. She wanted to do the right thing, the best thing, for Sloane.

But it had been a long time since she'd found a man attractive, and an even longer time since she'd been in a romantic environment with one. You couldn't get much more romantic than a sunflower farm at sunset, at least in Gabby's mind. Other women could have their Caribbean cruises and their white-tablecloth, expensive restaurants. Give her a pretty farm any day.

She guessed she was a farm girl, too, just like Sloane. Her daughter.

She took a deep breath in, let it out, and looked at Noah. "So…you wanted to talk?"

"Yes. Let's walk and talk," he said. "We need to make some decisions before your relationship with Sloane goes much further."

"Last call for the sunflower maze!" the hayride driver called as he pulled his tractor alongside the benches where they'd been sitting.

She glanced over at Noah. "Would you want to walk and talk in the sunflower maze?" Then she lowered her eyes. It was the kind of harebrained idea Todd had always criticized her for. Silly girl stuff.

But Noah raised an eyebrow and smiled. "I'd love to. Allow me." He stood and held out his arm, playacting an old-fashioned courtly gentleman.

She took his arm and then realized she shouldn't have. When she felt his strength, she wanted to cling on.

They climbed onto the hay wagon. Two couples joined them, one an older and probably long-married couple, and the other a pair of teenagers, maybe seventeen or eighteen.

"This is a romantic trip," their driver called back to them as he put the vehicle into gear. "Sunset, flowers, privacy… gentlemen, if you don't take advantage of this environment, you're losing an opportunity."

"Hear! Hear!" said the silver-haired gentleman. He leaned over and kissed his wife's cheek.

The teenagers cuddled closer together.

Gabby wanted to sink through the wagon's wooden floor. The last thing she and Noah needed was romance.

As the wagon pulled off, bouncing along the rutted road, they were jounced into each other. "Sorry," Noah said. "And, sorry about the romance angle. I didn't know that would happen."

"Live and learn," she said. It was getting to be their catch-phrase.

They rode past what seemed like miles of multicolored zinnias, and then a cornfield, golden from the rays of the setting sun. Finally, they jolted to a halt beside the sunflower maze. "Entrance is here," the driver said. "I'll pick you up at the end in an hour. See that you find your way!"

They entered the maze with the other two couples, joking about sending up smoke signals if anyone got lost. By unspoken agreement, the three couples went in different directions at the first fork.

The sunflowers ranged from shoulder-height to way above their heads. Many were the traditional gold color, but some were more exotic varieties of orange and brown.

Gabby and Noah walked for a few minutes, discussing the turns as they came to them. The other couples' voices drifted to them and they caught an occasional glimpse of them through the sunflowers' thick stalks. But mostly it felt isolated and beautiful and, yes, romantic.

"Now see," he said, looking around, "if I were using this maze in a thriller, we'd be running from a bad guy right about now."

"Ooh, that would be good. A unique environment for a chase scene."

"Right. Corn mazes and hedge networks have been done, but I've never seen a sunflower maze in my genre." He pulled out his phone and did a quick 360-degree video.

She liked that Noah had agreed to do the maze. Liked how he was as a father. Liked his creativity.

"Enough of that," he said, pocketing his phone. "We need to talk about our situation."

Here it came. Fun over, time for business. "We do," she agreed.

"How are you feeling about it, now that a few days have passed? Do you have any idea of whether you might want to, well, co-parent Sloane with me on some level?"

She looked up at the darkening sky, where a few stars twinkled. *What do I do, God?*

She wasn't one to claim she heard direct instructions from above. But she did sometimes get a strong feeling.

Right now, what she felt was *love*. It was God's command that they love one another. And, oh, how she wanted to express her love for Sloane, express it in direct action by taking care of her, teaching her, mothering her.

She wasn't sure it was the best thing. She was terrified her ex would find out. But when she pictured Sloane in her mind, Gabby couldn't turn down the opportunity to help with her. "What were you thinking?" she asked. "I know some divorced parents who split up weeks and weekends."

His brow wrinkled. "I wouldn't go that far," he said. "I'm kind of accustomed to spending most of my free time with her, and she's used to that, too. I wouldn't want her to be gone for a whole weekend, let alone a week."

"Then…would you want me to take her to do some things alone? Just, like, activities, for an afternoon or a day?"

"Maybe," he said. "But…to start, we could do a few things together, just the three of us."

Gabby thought about that. Imagined hanging out with Sloane and Noah, visiting a park together, sharing a meal, taking a hike. Like Noah had said, just the three of them.

Hmm.

"I can see how that would be a good thing for Sloane, but…" She trailed off. How to say what she wanted to say. "Look, just to be clear—" she started.

"I'm not in the market for—" he said at the same time. Then he smiled, just slightly. "You first."

"I just wanted to be clear that I'm not able to become a real family, if that was on your mind," she said. "I mean, you're a great guy…"

"And I'm not in the market for dating or marriage, because I need to keep things stable for Sloane. I hope this will work out, but we have to take it slow. I'm not the marrying kind, not anymore."

"Good," she said, "because I don't trust men."

They looked at each other and laughed awkwardly. "I'm glad we got *that* straightened out," Noah said.

"Same." She strolled on, and he walked beside her.

"So," he said after awhile, "you're off men because of your ex?"

She nodded. "He pretty much extinguished the urge." Even as she said it, she wasn't sure that was still true. But that was for another day's analysis. "What about you? You must have been the marrying kind at one point."

"I was cured of it, also," he said.

They rounded a corner and came to the silver-haired couple, kissing on a bench.

"Sorry!" Gabby exclaimed, stepping back.

"No problem, dear," the woman said, her cheeks pink, "but will you take our picture?"

"Of course." Gabby took the man's phone and took several shots, then handed it back.

It must be nice to have someone to grow old with.

They wandered on until they couldn't hear the others'

voices anymore. The maze was entirely shaded now, and Gabby shivered. "Getting a little chilly," she said.

Noah put an arm around her. "For chivalry's sake," he said, smiling.

She couldn't resist nestling into his warmth. "I appreciate that," she said.

They walked on, slowly. She looked up at him just as he looked at her and their eyes met. Their faces were close, and it was definitely romantic here. Was he going to kiss her? And what was this new, breathless part of herself that wanted him to?

She looked down, her face heating up. She'd just told him she wasn't interested in a relationship. He wasn't, either. They had something important to do together, and it would work best if it wasn't muddied up with romantic feelings engendered by a sunflower maze and a darkening sky and two bodies pressed just a little too close together for simple friendship.

Taking a deep breath, she stepped away from the shelter of his arm. Funny, she didn't feel cold at all anymore. She felt all too warm.

This was going to be interesting, parenting Sloane together.

Chapter Ten

Noah rode in the passenger seat of Gabby's little SUV, headed away from the sunflower farm. He'd shaken off whatever absurd feeling he'd had, a feeling that had caused him to put his arm around her. A feeling that had made him want to kiss her.

Thankfully, his walls had snapped back into place. That was how it should be, with the woman he was starting to trust with his daughter's safety and care. He cast about for a neutral topic of conversation. "Kind of nice to be the passenger," he said, looking around appreciatively. The fields were moonlit, bright enough that trees and buildings made shadows.

"A lot of men prefer to drive." Gabby signaled, then turned a corner.

"Your ex?" he guessed.

She nodded. "He would never let me drive. It got to a point where he didn't even want me to have car keys."

"Wow. That must have been rough." Noah struggled to keep his tone even. He had a big moral objection to men who controlled women.

"It was, especially when I was nine months pregnant."

Noah's fist clenched. He forced himself to relax. "That's

just plain dangerous, unless you have someone nearby who can help."

"Actually," she said, "that's just what happened. I started having contractions, and I got my neighbor to drive me to the farthest hospital she could. I registered as a Jane Doe, had Sloane, and left."

"Left the hospital?"

"Left the state." She signaled, then passed another car. She was playing it cool and seemed to be in control, but he noticed that her grip on the steering wheel had tightened. "It was the hardest thing I ever did, but I knew it would be better for my baby if she never even met my ex."

"Wow." He was sad for her, but impressed. "That took guts."

She shrugged. "Some would put me down for it. I mean, I basically abandoned my baby."

The forced flippancy in her tone just about broke his heart. "Did you really abandon her, though? You went through legal channels, I assume."

"I did." She slowed, made a turn. "When you're in labor, there's a lot of downtime. In the interludes between contractions, I asked for a social worker and explained the situation. Signed the paperwork saying I was giving up my..." She paused, and swallowed audibly. "My parental rights."

"You didn't abandon Sloane," he said gently. "You placed her for adoption. In your circumstances, it made all the sense in the world." He watched her, studied her strong silhouette, the rapid blinking of her eyes that told him she was near tears. "Want me to drive?"

She cleared her throat. "I'm fine."

And she was, he thought, watching her signal and carefully and confidently pass a slow-moving truck. She could drive while telling an emotional story.

She'd been through so much, and it had toughened her. She was incredibly strong.

And he'd almost kissed her. Even after they'd both said it wasn't a date.

He'd gotten a sense that she was open to it, just for a moment there. And then, wiser than he was, she'd stepped away.

The important thing was, she'd agreed to go for it with Sloane. She was willing to tell Sloane that she was her birth mother, and she was willing to try co-parenting. It was more than he had ever dreamed would happen when he'd moved here. It was the best-case scenario.

"So, where do we go from here?" she asked. They were getting close to Chesapeake Corners now. "What's the next step? Do we just blunder into Dee's place tonight and tell her?"

"No. We should think it through and figure out the right time, given her issues," he said.

A text pinged in. Dee. He opened it.

Sloane's falling asleep. Mind if I put her to bed at your place and hang out in your living room until you get home?

Perfect. Thank you. He looked over at Gabby. "I think we should research how to tell kids big secrets like this. There's expert advice available about everything now."

"When?"

"How about now?" He explained that Dee was putting Sloane to bed. "I know it's late. But I'm kind of a night owl. Have to be, to get stuff done as a single dad."

She tilted her head and then glanced over at him. "Okay, sure. I don't have to get up early. I can go to the late church service tomorrow."

They rode the rest of the way home in silence, but Noah's

mind raced. He questioned his own motives. Yes, he wanted to research the right way to talk to Sloane about this new facet of her adoption. He could use Gabby's help with that, and as busy as they both were, there wouldn't be a lot of opportunities. Working together tonight made sense.

Except he was now going to spend even more time with Gabby. Late-night time. He was playing with fire, and getting burned was a distinct possibility.

Half an hour later, they'd said goodbye to Dee. He'd checked on Sloane, and Gabby had run to her place to get her laptop. Now, they sat at his dining room table, both scouring the internet for ideas.

"Surprises aren't the best thing for kids," she said. "What I'm reading here confirms it." She bit her lip. "We should— I should—have made it an open adoption."

He reached out and touched her hand, briefly. "You did the best you could at the time." He still couldn't get over that she'd run away from an abusive husband while nine months pregnant. Actually, while she was in labor. "I really admire you."

She was looking at her computer again, but there were two high spots of color in her cheeks. Had his words made her happy or uncomfortable?

She was tapping keys. "We should expect that she might act out," she said.

He snorted. "It's Sloane. Of course she'll act out."

"Of course." Their eyes met in mutual amusement.

Noah's heart seemed to expand in his chest.

He'd never had that before: someone who cared for his daughter as much as he did, someone who found her dramatic ways fun as well as exasperating. He had not even experienced this kind of connection with his wife in the early days. Instead, he'd always felt kind of apologetic when they were discussing Sloane. Like it was his fault for wanting kids and for suggesting adoption.

They decided to watch for an occasion to tell her, maybe just prior to next weekend, so she'd have a couple of days to process it before going back to school.

Gabby closed her laptop.

Noah didn't want the evening to end. "Would you like some tea? I'm having some."

She checked the time. "It's after midnight. I should go."

"Do you have to?"

She looked up quickly, her expression uneasy but curious.

The old-fashioned kitchen clock ticked. Noah stood, reached for her hands, and helped her to her feet. Once she was standing, he didn't let go. "Thank you for being such a good partner in all this. I can't tell you what it means to me."

"We're doing well together," she said.

She wasn't pulling away. Her hair smelled like flowers, making it hard to think.

She looked up at him with speculation in her eyes.

Did that mean what he thought it meant? He was out of practice with reading women's signals. And he didn't want to make a move that would be unwelcome. A good relationship with Gabby was too important. "Back in the maze," he said, "I wanted to kiss you. Would you have let me?"

A smile tugged the corner of her very pretty mouth. "Maybe," she said, her voice teasing.

"Should we try again?"

"Maybe," she said again, raising an eyebrow.

He definitely liked this playful, teasing side of her. "Let's do," he said, and lowered his lips to hers.

Gabby had kissed a few guys in her life, but it had been a while. She thought she'd be rusty at it. As it turned out, though, she wasn't. She leaned into Noah's kiss, relishing the feeling of being held by him.

He stroked a hand down her hair. "You're a beautiful woman," he said, "inside and out." His fingers tangled in her hair and he kissed her again, deeper this time.

She could feel Noah's restraint in the careful way he held her. He wasn't the kind of guy who'd push for all he could get.

Her heart pounded and it was hard to catch her breath, but she didn't want this good feeling to stop. It was amazing to feel close to and protected by a man. So good to let up on her own sense of having to control everything. So good not to have to worry.

She closed her eyes and inhaled. He smelled good, woodsy, maybe from aftershave or from being outdoors.

Something nudged at her. What if this went on? What if Todd found out?

She might be making a really big mistake.

But she still felt more excited than worried. Like she was going on an adventure, something new and a little dangerous and wildly, wonderfully good.

She should be careful. She was a mother, after all. A mother trying to do the best thing possible for her child, the child she'd just found again after thinking she was lost forever.

Sloane should be the whole focus here, not whatever this *thing* was that was building between them.

But Noah was something else, a unique man who was raising Gabby's child alone and doing it well despite all the challenges. Noah had listened to her story and accepted it, even admired her for what she'd done in placing Sloane for adoption.

After all the years of self-recrimination, his kindness and approval felt like balm to her sore heart.

She stood on tiptoes to get closer to him, and this time, his kiss stopped her from thinking about anything at all. She could only feel. Being wrapped in his arms, knowing he wanted her, trusting him not to take things too far…it was like a beautiful, healing medicine.

After another minute, he gently put his hands on her shoulders and stepped back. "Much as I would like for this to go on," he said, "I can't. We both know where it could go, and that shouldn't happen."

"Daddy?" The voice calling from the back bedroom dissipated the romantic haze around them. Gabby took a couple of big steps backward.

That was the reality check. They couldn't have Sloane see them kissing. Couldn't lead her to have expectations that would never come to fruition.

"I'll sneak out," she whispered. She grabbed her laptop and backed toward the door as Noah turned toward Sloane's room.

She slipped out and headed for her cottage, unable to keep a big smile off her face.

Gabby spent Sunday thinking about Noah's kiss. No matter how often she told herself to quit acting like a lovesick teenager, she couldn't seem to let it go.

It wasn't so much excitement—well, it *was* that. But more, it was the safety she'd felt in his arms. He'd touched her so tenderly, and when she remembered the way his hand had tangled in her hair, the gentle brush of his thumb on her cheek, her stomach tightened and her whole chest warmed. After what she'd gone through in her marriage, she'd never expected to thrill at a man's kiss again.

Alongside the thrill, though, was fear. This could be dangerous. This could turn out badly.

Partly, the fear was that her heart would be broken. Partly, it was that Todd would locate her, discover she cared for someone else, and…well, what he would do was something she didn't even want to imagine.

Noah had said he could protect her. But he didn't know Todd, didn't know what he was capable of, didn't know how he reacted when thwarted or rejected.

And the idea that Sloane could be the target of his anger… it didn't bear thinking about.

If she played it cool and stayed away and backed off, though, would she be throwing away the chance for a kind of happiness she'd never dared to dream about?

Finally, after praying about it in church, she decided to take a middle ground. She'd act friendly, but not romantic. Focus on Sloane, who, after all, was the most important person in this situation.

And she'd try to trust that God had this, that He was in control.

It was Sunday evening when she realized that Noah hadn't noticed she was playing it cool, because he hadn't attempted to get in touch.

She thought about that during a long walk with Caramel, and her pace got faster and faster, like she could outrun her feelings, outrun Noah, outrun all men who pretended they were less emotional than women while really being way more unpredictable and volatile.

She shouldn't feel that way. Noah didn't owe her anything. He'd kissed her; so what? A sophisticated woman would call it a product of the situation in which they'd found themselves, laugh it off, and let it go.

But Gabby wasn't sophisticated. She was a second-grade teacher who lived in a small town. Sure, she had some intense stuff and some pain in her background, but for the most part, she was simple and inexperienced. Kissing a man meant something to her.

Apparently it didn't mean anything to Noah.

She saw a couple up ahead, holding hands, and blew out a disgusted breath. She picked up Caramel and headed home at race-walking pace.

Sloane didn't come to reading club on Monday as Gabby had hoped she would. But Gabby wasn't going to push it. They had a plan to talk to Sloane and let her know the truth on Friday after school. Until then, there was no need for extra interactions with Sloane and Noah.

She was getting her mail at the central mailbox station after dinner when she saw Sloane and Noah emerge from their cottage and head toward the mailboxes.

Play it cool, she reminded herself.

She pulled out her mail and started strolling back toward home, flipping through advertising circulars and bills to avoid giving too much attention to their approach.

And then she saw a letter with a handwritten address.

The handwriting was familiar. Too familiar.

Way too familiar.

Her hands shook as she tucked the letter underneath the bills.

How did Todd know her address?

"Hi, Miss Gabby!" Sloane bounced toward her.

"Hi, honey," she choked out. If he knew where Gabby lived, did he know about Sloane?

Noah met them in the middle of the road. His warm smile melted her heart.

So he hadn't been pushing her away or downplaying their kiss. He'd just been playing it cool, like she had. She couldn't help smiling back.

She shouldn't act like a silly, sensitive teenager. It was just that Noah made her feel like she was fifteen again.

And then she thought of the letter and her smile faded away. What did it say?

"Sloane and I have a proposition for you," Noah said.

"Uh, okay." *What does the letter say? What does he know?*

"Sloane wants to read with Caramel, but she's not ready to do it in the school book club. Would you be willing to meet with her for the occasional extra session after school?" He was looking at her as if he knew she'd say yes.

Which she would, of course, but…she tilted her head, studying him. Hadn't they decided not to make any changes until Friday?

He looked right back at her, and it seemed like hidden meanings were flying in the air between them, a whole swarm of them. "Are you okay?" he asked.

Okay about what? About telling Sloane the truth? About the letter that seemed to burn in her hands, even hidden amongst the bills? About their kiss?

"I'm fine," she said, and knew from his confused frown that she hadn't been convincing.

What did the letter say?

She wanted them both to leave so she could read it. Yet she also wanted to never read it, to throw it away, to keep his poison away from her.

"Could me and Caramel read now?" Sloane took her hand and looked up at her, her expression hopeful.

Well. Sloane asking to read was a bell ringer of an event. She glanced at Noah and saw his smile. He thought so, too.

"Of course you can, honey," she said to Sloane. "Let's get Caramel and you can read to her on the back porch."

"Yay!" Sloane threw her hands in the air in a V for *victory* and ran toward Gabby's cottage.

"Nice to see her so excited about reading," Noah commented. "But are you sure this is okay? You seem…preoccupied."

She should tell him why, tell him about the letter. And she would, after she'd had a chance to read it herself. "Long day," she said.

Of course, he saw through the bland excuse. His forehead wrinkled. She hated that she was making him worry, maybe even making him insecure. But she would clarify it all later.

"Come *on*," Sloane begged, running back toward them.

"Hold your horses, kiddo," Gabby said, using a phrase that always made her second graders laugh. It worked for Sloane, too. They said goodbye to Noah, who promised to pick Sloane up in half an hour. Then Gabby got Sloane settled on the back porch, Caramel beside her. "I can read to her by myself," Sloane said.

"Okay, honey." Gabby was curious how Sloane would do, but not as curious as she was about that letter. So once Sloane had picked a book and started sounding out words, she went inside, sitting at her kitchen table where she could see Sloane and Caramel through the door. She pulled out the letter, slit it open, and read it. Looked at the photo he'd enclosed, of the two of them together.

Then she slumped, resting her forehead on her clasped hands.

He'd made mistakes, he said. The past was the past. He wanted her back.

She shoved the photo and letter away. His smooth talk didn't fool her. The few times he'd contact her before, early on, it had been due to a lack of money or a breakup with a girlfriend. No doubt the same had happened now.

Even if he was contrite at the moment, he'd soon be upset with her again. Upset led to violence. There was no way.

She heard a crash on the back porch and looked up to

see Sloane standing. The book she'd been reading lay face down on the floor on the other side of the porch. She must have thrown it.

She hurried out. "What's wrong?"

"Reading is stupid," Sloane said. "Mommy told me that, and it's true."

Gabby was floored. "Your mom told you reading was stupid?"

"Yes, and Daddy's books are stupid." She lifted her chin and glared at Gabby.

Gabby stared back at her. Her mother had disrespected Noah's work, and shared that disrespect with their child? Did Noah know?

The woman had obviously been angry with Noah, but in expressing that to her child, she'd made Sloane hate books and reading.

Would any mother do a disservice like that to her child on purpose?

Caramel whined, sitting on the floor six feet away from Sloane. Gabby sat down beside the little dog and pulled her into her lap. "I think when you threw the book, it made Caramel scared," she told Sloane. "It's okay not to like a book, but it's not okay to throw it."

Sloane's mouth flattened. She sat back down on the porch couch, in the corner farthest away from Gabby and Caramel. She pulled her knees to her chest and looked away.

Gabby's thoughts whirled as she tried to process everything that had happened in the past hour.

There was a part of her that was starting to care for Noah—a lot. A part of her that wanted something to grow between them. But that wasn't safe, not for Sloane, not for Gabby, not for Noah. The letter she'd received had reminded her of that fact.

If Todd knew where she lived, he could show up anytime. She leaned back against an ottoman, petting Caramel.

Sloane was so vulnerable. Today had illustrated that. While she'd been excited about reading to Caramel, she hadn't been able to stick with it when it had gotten hard. Instead, she'd reverted back to her old point of view, that reading wasn't worth the trouble.

Now Gabby knew where at least some of that attitude had come from: Sloane's late mother. That meant it would be harder to eradicate.

The issues with reading could jeopardize Sloane's chances to succeed in school. Even worse, though, Todd could jeopardize Sloane's physical safety.

As her thoughts churned, Gabby couldn't help feeling that disaster was about to strike them all.

Chapter Eleven

Noah was whistling as he walked over to pick up Sloane. He was thrilled that she'd voluntarily put herself into a reading situation. Caramel was the reason. Well, Caramel and Gabby.

He sucked in his breath, thinking about what it had been like to kiss Gabby. A smile came to his face, a deep smile from the heart. He'd loved holding her. He'd loved that she was enthusiastic about kissing him. Getting close to her like that had been one of the sweetest moments of his life.

He tapped on the door of Gabby's place. "Anyone home?"

"We're here," Gabby called.

He walked in through the kitchen and out onto the back porch. "I have an idea," he said to Sloane. "Since you agreed to read with Caramel, how about if we check out the book-shop in town tonight? It's open, I checked."

Sloane had been crunched into a corner of the wicker couch, but now she sat up straighter. "And get ice cream?"

"Well," he said, "the bookshop *is* practically right next to the ice-cream shop."

"Can *she* go?" Sloane pointed at Gabby. "And Caramel?"

Noah wanted Gabby to go, too. She looked so cute in her after-school shorts and T-shirt, her hair piled into some kind of topknot. She wore flip-flops, revealing that she'd painted her toenails a new color. Pink this time.

He wasn't normally a fan of pink, but he liked it on Gabby. He'd like almost anything on Gabby.

"Caramel can't go, sweetie," she was saying. She was sitting on the floor, holding the little dog in her lap. "She's not allowed in the bookshop or the ice-cream shop."

Sloane narrowed her eyes. "I saw a dog in a store before."

"Some stores allow it," Gabby acknowledged. "And all stores have to let service dogs come in. Those are dogs trained to help someone with a disability, like someone who's blind."

"Caramel helps kids read."

"She does," Gabby said, "but she's a therapy dog, not a service dog. She's not essential to any of us getting to the store and walking around, so she has to stay home."

Sloane looked ready to argue. Uh-oh.

"Would you like to feed her dinner?" Gabby asked.

"Yeah!" Sloane jumped up. "Where's her food?"

"Slow down." Gabby was laughing. "I'll get it off the shelf and you can measure out a quarter of a cup."

Sloane hesitated, then nodded. "I can do that."

"Come on, then." Gabby walked to the kitchen, pulled out the measuring cups, and set them in a row. "Can you guess which is a quarter of a cup? Remember, that means four little ones can fit into one big one."

No surprise that Gabby made a teachable moment of it. She was great that way.

Sloane studied them. "That one's for Caramel," she said, pointing at the smallest cup.

"You're right! And see, it's *one quarter* the size of the full cup." Gabby held up the two sizes to show Sloane. Sloane nodded impatiently and reached for the smaller measuring cup. Gabby laughed and handed it to her, not belaboring the point. While Sloane carefully dipped out a quarter cup of kibble, Gabby flashed Noah a smile. "Can't help being a teacher, even in my off-hours. It's good for kids to be exposed to concepts like that over and over. Makes it easier for them to grasp it when math class comes along."

"I like it." Noah smiled back at her.

Their eyes met. Held.

"Does she get water, too?" Sloane asked.

"Yes, she does. You can dump out her old water and fill it up with fresh."

While Sloane did that, Gabby stepped closer to Noah, and he caught a whiff of something flowery from her hair. He inhaled, transported back to their kiss.

"So," she said, "it didn't actually go that well, the reading. She got frustrated."

"No tantrum, though?"

She held out a hand, tipping it from side to side in the *sort of* gesture. "She threw the book, but not at anyone and not real hard. I may have picked one that was a little too difficult for her."

He lifted his hands, palms up. "You tried. And we'll keep trying."

She smiled a little. "We will."

He wanted to stand close to her all night, to look into her eyes. But that wasn't going to happen with an active seven-year-old in the room, especially one who didn't and couldn't know that he and Gabby *liked* each other. Not yet, anyway. "I don't mean to push you into going to the bookshop," he said. "You don't have to come. I'm sure it's the last thing you want, hanging out with a seven-year-old after teaching them all day."

"Well, true, but...parents do that all the time, right? And anytime she's willing to go to a bookish place, I'd like to encourage that."

"Me, too." Another meeting of the eyes. Hers were so pretty. He could get lost in them.

Sloane ran over and threw her arms around him. "Can we go *now*?"

"We can," he said, "if it's okay with Gabby."

"*Miss* Gabby, Daddy," Sloane corrected him. Then she threw her arms around Gabby. "You're going!"

"I'm going," Gabby said, laughing. "Just let me get my purse and jacket."

While she did that and Sloane played with Caramel, Noah looked idly around her kitchen. It was the same as his, and yet not. There was a hanging plant over the sink, and red-and-white-checked curtains at the window. A row of canisters labeled *Flour* and *Sugar* must be her supplies for baking. There was a book open, face down, on the table, as if she'd been reading while she'd had dinner. He remembered the days before he'd become a parent when he'd been able to do that.

There was an envelope beside the book. He wasn't trying to read it, not really, but he couldn't miss the return address: Montana. A photograph was mostly hidden by the envelope, but when he caught a glimpse of blond hair, his instinctive nosiness made him nudge the envelope aside.

There was Gabby. A younger Gabby, but not that much younger. She was leaning against a really good-looking man—movie-star handsome—astride a motorcycle. Gabby wore leathers and a big smile.

Noah covered the photo back up, his mind racing. Gabby had said she was miserable in her marriage, that her husband was abusive. Was *this* the abusive husband? And why did Gabby look happy in the picture if so?

Was the business about her bad ex just a ploy or an exaggeration? If the marriage wasn't bad, or not that bad, then why on earth had she given up Sloane? Did she really want kids? Would she really be a good mom to Sloane, or was she like his wife, likely to bug out at the first sign of trouble? Was she a liar, too?

Beneath those questions, something else churned. Something he didn't want to feel. Something ugly.

He was self-aware enough to recognize the mix of jealousy and possessiveness and insecurity that had risen in him when he'd seen the picture of Gabby, laughing with her good-looking biker husband.

How could he, an average-looking nerdy writer, measure up? Even if the relationship with Gabby progressed, how far could it go before she tired of him and sought companionship elsewhere?

"Ready," Gabby called.

They went out and piled into his SUV. Gabby and Sloane seemed happy and excited, chattering away with one another about their favorite flavors of ice cream.

Noah was preoccupied, his mind racing. He had to force himself to concentrate on the road during the short drive to the center of town.

He still felt guilty, terribly guilty, that he'd let his late wife mistreat Sloane. Was he making the same mistake again, with Gabby? Was he being led by his hormones, his strong attraction to Gabby?

Maybe she wasn't the woman she appeared to be.

At the bookshop, he was distracted. The proprietor pressed him to commit to a signing, and he nodded and accepted the suggested date, even though he wasn't sure he was free then. Sloane ran around the store and found a stuffed toy, and he bought it for her instead of a book.

As they left, Gabby was looking at him funny. But what was the deal with her and her smiling, good-looking husband? What kind of person was she?

Or, what kind of person was *he*? Was he just a jealous jerk? There could be all kinds of explanations for that photo.

He'd been excited to help Sloane with reading, but he couldn't focus. His mind swirled with confusion.

He bought ice cream for the two of them mechanically, turned it down for himself, and drove home while they ate, ignoring Sloane's request to sit in front of the ice cream shop and eat it, and risking getting ice cream all over his leather seats.

"You okay?" Gabby asked quietly as they all got out of the SUV.

"Fine," he said. He waved, impersonally, and turned toward the house, shepherding Sloane in front of him.

Not before he glimpsed a hurt expression on Gabby's face.

Two hours ago, he'd been happy about everything: Gabby's presence in his and Sloane's lives, Sloane's improved behavior, the prospect of getting closer to Gabby living here in a small town. He'd been excited about what the future might hold. He'd felt good about himself, like he was worthy of having this mega-improvement in his and Sloane's lives.

Now, he felt small and insecure and closed-in. Defensive, as if he needed to toughen up and stop himself from caring.

He needed to focus his care on Sloane. He needed to vet any new person in her life very, very carefully, not rush into a connection with someone he'd only known, when it came down to it, a couple of weeks. Not even.

Noah could feel himself putting up walls. It was familiar, the comfortable thing to do. The tendency had hurt his marriage. It might very well spell the end of any romantic possibilities between him and Gabby.

No more kissing.

He tightened his stomach against the pain of that idea. He

needed to toughen up. He had a lot of thinking to do before he went forward with the plan of revealing the truth about Gabby to Sloane.

On Wednesday night, Gabby feigned interest in her book club's discussion at the library, but apparently, it didn't work. As the group broke up and people clustered around the refreshment table, Aunt Dee grabbed her arm and gently tugged her off to the side of the room.

"Don't you want a cookie?" she asked her aunt. "Peanut butter blossoms. Your favorite."

"I want you to tell me what's wrong. I know you, and you're usually outspoken in your opinions at book club. Tonight, you've barely said a word."

Busted. They headed into the hall, and Gabby paused outside the children's section. "I was going to stop and grab a couple of books for Sloane, but…oh, I don't know."

Aunt Dee studied her. "It's not like you to be indecisive. Do you want to stop or not?"

Gabby blew out a sigh. "I was going to try to find a couple of books about adoption, to help with explaining things to Sloane. But now I don't know what to do." She walked past the entryway to the children's section, slowly, barely paying attention to where she was going.

"Come on. Let's talk." Her aunt took her elbow and propelled her out to the library's porch overlooking the town's main street. They found two adjacent rocking chairs off to the side and settled in.

Evening sun flooded the street and shop windows in a golden light. Someone was walking a Rottweiler from one direction, and another person was walking a Chihuahua from the other. Gabby vaguely knew the Chihuahua's owner and watched to see if intervention was needed, but the two dogs just sniffed each other while the owners chatted, and then all of them walked on.

Gabby sat back down and fluffed her hair off her warm neck. "Hot out here."

Aunt Dee made a circling gesture with her hand. "Come on, out with it. What's got you so distracted?"

It could only help to talk with Aunt Dee, who knew so much of the background. Gabby had been going over and over it in her head since Monday night, and had failed to reach a conclusion. Maybe her wise aunt's perspective would help her know what to do next.

She drew in a breath. "We—Noah and I—are supposed to talk to Sloane on Friday after school, let her know the truth about the adoption and our connection. But I'm having doubts."

"Real doubts? Or are you just being wimpy?"

Gabby smiled a little. "Real, unfortunately." She told her aunt about the letter she'd received from her ex.

Aunt Dee blew out a sigh and shook her head slowly, back and forth. "Wow. Do you think he's sincere in wanting to get back together?"

Gabby lifted her hands, palms up. "Who knows? It's possible, but it's more likely he's just trying to mess with me. The scary part is, he knows where I live now."

Her aunt winced. "Wonder how he found out."

Gabby shook her head. "There are so many ways these days. I'm surprised he hasn't done it before. In fact, that makes me worried..." She trailed off, not wanting to voice her fear.

"That he could find out something about Noah and Sloane. Could you get a restraining order?"

Gabby had thought of that, but had dismissed it almost immediately. "He could get around it, if they'd even give me one," she said. "And you can't have one forever. Noah can't have one against a person he's never even met, nor can Sloane, so…" She leaned forward and let her face fall into her hands. "This is why I placed Sloane for adoption, to protect her, and now…" She turned her head to the side, still propped on her hands, facing her aunt.

Dee nodded, sighing heavily. "It's a real concern."

"It is. And once I tell Sloane I'm her birth mother, it's a lifelong commitment. No way could I give her up again. I can't put her through it, and I don't think I could survive it myself."

"Oh, honey." Aunt Dee patted her arm. "I'm sorry it's so complicated."

They sat rocking, not talking. Gabby's mind was racing. It did feel good to talk about it, but obviously her aunt didn't have an easy answer. There wasn't one.

Gabby should never have married Todd. She'd seen enough signs of what he was like after they'd been dating a few months. But she'd been like a pathetic, fawning puppy, especially since Todd had been so skilled at convincing her she was almost good enough. She'd thought that, if she just tried harder, she could make the abuse stop.

She shouldn't have been that way. It wasn't as if she'd had a horrible childhood. Her parents had been preoccupied, sure, but they had cared about her, came to some of her school events, made sure she had food and clothing. A better person would have taken her very decent childhood and turned it into a sound base for growth.

Instead, she'd let the family's declining social status, and her own insecurity about her looks and appeal, lead her into a miserable danger zone that had put not only her, but also her child, at risk.

"I was a fool to get involved with him," she said, her stomach clenching.

Her aunt looked over at her as she rocked. "Most of us have made some unwise choices due to love. Sometimes, it turns out okay. Sometimes, it leads to a few years of unhappiness, or even a lot of years." She patted Gabby's arm. "And sometimes, it leads to danger and violence. You were one of those, but I don't think you can blame yourself for his actions."

Gabby looked into her aunt's wise eyes, and despite her worries, her heart filled with love and gratitude. "Thank you for being so good to me."

"Oh, honey," Aunt Dee said. "The gratitude is mutual."

Doves cooed from somewhere above them. A family came out of the library, the kids running and yelling with the freedom, the adults holding stacks of picture books. Late-blooming lilies cast a nighttime fragrance. Gabby took deep breaths, trying to soak in the peace of her surroundings.

"Have you talked to Noah about the new development?" Aunt Dee asked.

Gabby leaned her head back against the wooden rocker. "Noah's acting weird."

"How so?"

"Just…cold. Distant."

Several of the book club ladies emerged from the library, still talking with animation about tonight's book. A gentle breeze broke through the September heat.

Gabby thought of how Noah had avoided her eyes when they'd encountered each other in the driveway. How he'd waved, but had not come over, when she'd arrived home from school and had seen him sitting outside.

"He's changed, and I don't know why," she said.

Aunt Dee tilted her head to one side. "He sure seemed

friendly when I left the two of you at the sunflower farm on Saturday."

Gabby's face heated. "He *was* friendly, then."

Aunt Dee shrugged. "He's probably just being a man. Stifling his emotions. You need to address this Todd situation with him, I think."

She probably did, but…he'd kissed her, and then seemed to reject her. Hadn't he liked their kiss? Had he decided, upon reflection, that she wasn't appealing to him, just as her ex had done?

Her insecurities just added to the huge, impossible conflict she felt. She wanted to be a mother to Sloane, wanted it with all her heart. At the same time, she was terrified of what Todd might do. She was also scared of the long-term connection with Noah, who seemed suddenly ambivalent toward her. Was she headed for heartbreak, or worse?

"Find a time to talk to him," Aunt Dee said firmly. "I'll take care of Sloane."

"You don't have to do that," Gabby protested.

"She's my niece, and you know as well as I do that we don't have a whole lot of relatives. I want to." She stood. "Come on, it's getting late and we should head home."

They walked through town toward the cottage resort. Mechanically, Gabby greeted the people they passed.

It had helped her, talking with Aunt Dee. And she knew the woman was wise, and right.

She had to talk with Noah. But she wasn't looking forward to it. Spending time with him would be awkward at best, since he ran so hot and cold toward her.

If she just backed out now, backed out of Noah's and Sloane's lives, Sloane would be safe. Noah would find someone else, maybe.

Gabby would be devastated for life.

And maybe Sloane wouldn't be okay. She'd gotten close with Gabby. She might feel abandoned if Noah and Gabby parted ways. She might regress. Gabby hated the thought of causing Sloane to backslide.

On the other hand, maybe she was deluding herself. Kids these days had lots of adults in and out of their lives, teachers and caregivers and neighbors. Sloane might miss Gabby for a week or two, but then forget all about her.

The thought made Gabby's heart heavy, as if a huge stone were pressing down on her chest.

Gabby wanted to mother Sloane, wanted it desperately now that the little girl had embedded herself so deeply in her heart.

But if they went forward with the co-parenting idea and Todd found out, they could all be literally killed.

Her stomach churned.

There was no answer, she realized, as she bid her aunt goodnight. No single, perfect answer.

And this wasn't something she could decide on her own. Other people were involved.

Okay then. She'd talk to Noah as soon as possible and find out what he was thinking and how he wanted to proceed.

And she'd pray about it. Maybe God had an answer she just wasn't seeing.

Chapter Twelve

The text from Gabby came in on Thursday just a few minutes after Noah saw her car pull in at the end of the school day. We need to talk.

And yeah, he was aware of when she came and went. He didn't want to be, but he was.

Agreed, he texted back. Now? Dee said she can watch Sloane.

Oh, so Gabby had taken that on herself, to decide when their talk would take place and find Sloane a babysitter? That was a little annoying. What if he'd been busy?

But of course, he wasn't busy, not if Sloane was safe with Dee. And he had to admit that he wanted to talk with Gabby for all kinds of reasons.

Twenty minutes later, they were walking toward the waterfront at Gabby's suggestion.

The late afternoon sun slanted down, casting a golden hue over the town. A slight breeze from the bay carried that distinctive saltwater scent, cooling the sun's heat. The smell of hydrangeas filled the air. Squirrels ran and played in the little park they walked through, both drawn toward the boardwalk and the bay.

In another world, this setting would be romantic. But not

here. Not now. "I saw you had a letter from your ex," he said abruptly.

She stopped, turned, stared at him. "You did? When?"

"Monday night, when Sloane was reading with you and Caramel." He forked his fingers through his hair, pushing it back, feeling hot and uncomfortable despite the pleasant weather.

"Wow, I didn't know I'd left it out," she said. "Did you read it?"

"No. I didn't want to invade your privacy."

She nodded. "Thank you. I hate that he knows my address. It worries me that he could find me so easily." She didn't tell him what was in the letter.

"Are you thinking about going back to him?" The words burst out of his mouth, much less eloquent and far more emotional than the calm discussion he'd envisioned.

He started walking again, but she stayed where she was, and when he turned back, she was staring at him. "Why on earth would you think that?" she asked.

"You looked happy in the picture," he said, taking a couple of steps back toward her.

"You saw that?" She sounded shocked.

Aha. "Feeling guilty?" he asked.

"No." She started walking then, her pace fast enough that he had to take long steps to catch up. "You saw all that," she said. "And you didn't tell me? What, you think I was lying all this time, saying he was dangerous?"

"Well…"

"Why do you suddenly not believe me, Noah?"

"Because he's a great-looking man, and you looked happy. You looked good together."

She shook her head vehemently. "That's what makes him so dangerous," she said. "No one thinks he's a bad guy. He's charming, too, or he can be," she added, her tone bitter. "Even Sloane would probably like him at first."

Noah felt a pang. Would Sloane like her birth father better than she liked him?

"But he's evil, Noah. Evil. And now he knows where I live."

They walked a few minutes while he processed all that, trying to decide whether he believed her. "Are you suggesting we just back off the whole thing?"

She didn't answer, but he heard a choked sound. When he looked over, he was shocked to see tears, real tears, streaming down her face.

"Do you want to call it off?" he said, pushing forward.

"I want to be her mother more than anything," she sputtered, "now that it's been held out to me." She gulped and went on. "And yet, if it puts her at risk… I just don't know what to do."

Compassion tugged at him, pushing aside his foolish jealousy. "Come here." He took her arm and guided her to a bench that faced out onto the bay. A passing kid on a skateboard looked at them curiously. Noah frowned to keep the kid away.

Her obvious strong emotion pushed him toward believing her. And if she was telling the truth…well, the guy couldn't be that dangerous, could he?

If it was just a physical danger, not an emotional one, he could handle anything the guy threw out. It wasn't cockiness on his part, or at least, he didn't think so. It was just trusting his own skills and experience. He could keep them all safe. But he knew she didn't believe that, so as he sat down next to her, he said, "We can get the police involved."

"Not if he doesn't do anything illegal," she said. "And he knows that, so he won't. Not at first."

She was swallowing hard, and he couldn't let her obvious

pain go uncomforted. He put an arm around her and tugged her next to him. "We'll figure this out," he said, though he didn't really know how.

The temptation was to kiss her. And in her vulnerable state, she might let him.

But he couldn't take advantage of that. And he was still having doubts.

His wife had acted like she wanted to be a mother, had cried with her desire for it, but it had proven not to be the case. He'd believed her because he'd wanted to be with her.

Later, when he'd seen signs of her infidelity, she'd made up credible stories to lure Noah back to her side. The fake affection with which she'd convinced him turned his stomach. Not only that, but he felt like a fool.

Was the same scenario playing out again? Were his hormones making him believe in Gabby's sincerity?

"I *think* we should go forward," he said, but he could hear the uncertainty in his own voice. And she heard it, too—he could tell. She pulled away and studied him.

He couldn't keep the confusion and doubt off his face. He'd never been a good liar.

She sighed. "You're giving me mixed messages. Let's sleep on it and reconnect tomorrow."

As they walked home, not talking, he thought about what she'd said. It could all be true, about her ex, or she could be exaggerating—or worse.

He wanted to co-parent with Gabby. Wanted to do more than that, if the truth be known. And his natural inclination was to move forward, not to bumble around in fear of some nebulous enemy who was probably more than halfway across the country.

But there was Sloane to consider. If Gabby wasn't reliable, he had to keep her tender heart safe.

Why had he thought this would be easy?

"Look," he said, "the more I think about it, the more I think we should postpone telling her."

She looked at him quickly, saw something in his face, and looked away. "Okay," she said tonelessly.

He had the sense that he'd hurt her deeply with that response. That this discussion hadn't really fixed anything.

He walked her to her door and she went inside without speaking or looking at him. Her shoulders slumped.

Either she was a great actor, or she was devastated. He didn't know which would be worse.

After the school day ended on Friday, Gabby drove home and went directly into her cottage.

She didn't even glance in the direction of Noah's cottage. This was the day they were supposed to tell Sloane the truth, and then he'd changed his mind. She felt her opportunity to mother Sloane slipping away, and her insides were scraped raw by the loss.

After changing into shorts and flip-flops, she took Caramel outside. While the dog did her business, Gabby looked around the yard and noticed that her flowers were drooping. It was unseasonably hot for September. She got the hose and watered them while she waited for Caramel to finish sniffing every bush and rock.

A screen door slammed, and Sloane came running over, looking so adorable in her white shorts and purple shirt that Gabby's heart clutched at the sight.

"Can I play with Caramel?" Sloane was already kneeling by the dog, scratching her ears.

"If it's okay with your dad."

"It is," Sloane assured her.

Was it, though? Sighing, Gabby sent Noah a quick text asking him.

As long as she stays in sight, he texted back.

Didn't he even think he should come out and check in with his daughter? Was he that intent on staying away from Gabby?

She hooked Caramel up to her leash and reminded Sloane to stay where she could see Gabby.

"I will! Come on, Car-Car!" And they were off.

Gabby watched, smiling but also aching inside. Having a child to play with was great for Caramel, with her small-dog energy. And having a dog around seemed to suit Sloane, too.

How long could it go on, though? How long until Noah and Sloane moved away and left Gabby's life forever?

It was hard to imagine how she'd filled her days before the pair of them had moved in next door. In such a short time, they'd become integral to her happiness.

And now Todd, even from a distance, had taken them away from her.

She turned the hose onto her row of dahlias, reflecting. There had been no follow-up contact, no phone calls or emails from her ex. The letter she'd received from him seemed like a bad dream.

But yet, it had had its impact. Noah had seen it, and it had caused him to pull back from letting Gabby reveal the truth to Sloane. Even though that was the whole reason he'd come to Chesapeake Corners, he seemed to now think that there was a risk she'd go back to her ex.

It was ridiculous. She'd had to fight so hard to leave the man; why on earth would she ruin her life by going back?

If only he hadn't seen that picture. Todd *was* movie-star handsome, and that could give any ordinary-looking guy an insecure feeling.

Except that Noah was good-looking in his way, and so much better of a person. He had so many accomplishments to his name. How could he possibly be intimidated by her ex's empty, shallow good looks?

It didn't make sense, so maybe that wasn't the real issue. Maybe, upon reflection, he'd realized he didn't want to be permanently involved with Gabby through co-parenting Sloane. Maybe the ex thing was just an excuse.

After all, *she* wasn't so amazingly good-looking. She was too wholesome to be very appealing to men, at least according to Todd. Certainly, she didn't have a glamorous model's figure like Noah's ex must have had.

Misery wrapped around her like a suffocating blanket. Why had she opened her heart to Noah? Why had she let him kiss her? Let herself hope that it might go somewhere?

Gabby straightened her spine and shook her head to clear it. She needed to stop thinking all these negative thoughts. If Noah didn't want her, so be it, but maybe there was a way to salvage a relationship of some kind with Sloane.

She looked around and felt a jolt of worry when she didn't see either child or dog. Then she spotted them.

Sloane and Caramel had drifted over toward Mr. Kennedy's place. It was sweet how Sloane had gotten into the heart of the older man. And Gabby needed to get out of her useless rumination and do something for someone else.

She filled a big watering can and lugged it over toward Mr. Kennedy's cottage. She'd noticed, even from a distance, that his plants were droopier than hers were. It was the heat, but he was normally diligent about keeping things watered. He was the one who called Aunt Dee if he thought the common flower beds weren't being taken care of properly. Maybe he wasn't feeling well, or had gone away on a trip.

Sloane waved to Gabby and pointed toward the back of

Mr. Kennedy's place. Gabby nodded and waved, giving tacit permission.

Sloane loved to watch Mr. Kennedy fill his bird feeder, and sometimes he let her help with that important task. She also enjoyed visiting his hamster, Atticus, and looking through his wildlife books and photographs. He'd become a grandfather figure to Sloane, a calming, settling influence. That was a very good thing.

Gabby reached the cottage with her heavy watering can. As she watered Mr. Kennedy's tomatoes, Sloane came back around the cottage, holding Caramel in her arms. "Mr. Kennedy is weird," she said.

He was, Gabby supposed. "Weird is okay," she said. "We're all a little weird. What makes you say that now, though?"

"Come and see." Sloane reached out and took Gabby's hand.

The trusting gesture and the feel of that small hand in her own made Gabby's heart squeeze painfully. She would follow this sweet child anywhere. She put down her watering can and let Sloane lead her to the back of Mr. Kennedy's cottage.

"Look," Sloane said, pointing.

Mr. Kennedy was walking around his back porch. Or rather, weaving around. Gabby had never seen him so unsteady on his feet before.

She moved closer and noticed that his newspaper was scattered over the porch floor. A can of soda lay on its side on the end table beside his chair, its contents making a puddle on the indoor-outdoor carpet.

That wasn't like him. He was a neat person, almost obsessively so. Uneasy, she walked closer. "Hi, Mr. Kennedy. How are you today?"

"I'd be better if I could catch a glimpse of your pretty aunt," he said, his voice a little slurry.

Gabby blinked. Had he been drinking? She'd never heard him talk about Aunt Dee with romantic overtones before.

He lurched a little and grabbed onto a wall for balance. He clung to it, looking dazed. Looking like he was going to pass out.

Gabby's stomach tightened. "Go get your dad," she said to Sloane. "I think Mr. Kennedy is sick. We need to take him to the hospital."

Noah sat in the waiting room at the ER, Sloane beside him. Gabby sat on Sloane's other side.

They'd gotten Mr. Kennedy to Noah's SUV, steadying him in between them while Sloane ran ahead to open the door. Then Sloane had taken Caramel into Gabby's cottage while Noah and Gabby had talked to Mr. Kennedy, or tried to. He wasn't having pain anywhere and he said he hadn't been drinking. He just felt dizzy. And he was definitely confused.

Sloane had asked a million questions on the way to the hospital. What was wrong with Mr. Kennedy? Would he be okay? Should they stop and get him a snack, maybe some ice cream? Who would feed Atticus while he was at the hospital?

Then, when the ER workers had whisked Mr. Kennedy away, Sloane had gone silent. Gabby had found crayons and a coloring book somewhere, and was keeping Sloane occupied with them, but Sloane kept looking toward the door through which Mr. Kennedy had disappeared.

Poor kiddo. She'd lost her mom, and she was probably terrified, on some unconscious level, of losing someone else she cared about.

Noah was used to being in unpredictable and dangerous situations, especially during his time in the military. He'd learned long ago to stifle his emotions in order to accomplish what he needed to accomplish.

But he was also the creative type, and his emotions seemed to be getting closer to the surface every day. The sight of his elderly neighbor being wheeled away by medics had wrung his heart.

Mr. Kennedy was turning out to be a good friend. Definitely crotchety, but all bark and no bite. The way his face lit up when he saw Sloane, the way he asked her questions and actually listened to her rambling answers, had endeared him to Noah. Noah had started praying as he drove and hadn't stopped, a simple prayer: *Father, be with him and heal him.*

The waiting room was about half-full. Family and friend groups talked quietly. There were a couple of teenage boys wearing soccer uniforms there with a worried mom, who kept pacing back and forth. A father held a baby, rocking her gently; he kept looking toward the door into the patient treatment area.

So much fear in this room; so many hurting people. Noah expanded his prayer to include everyone in the ER, in the hospital.

The last time he'd been in an ER waiting room was when his wife had died. He'd managed to block out that horrible day for the most part, but being here was kicking up those memories. He'd gotten the call and rushed to the hospital, bringing Sloane along because he didn't have anyone to care for her. They'd arrived just after the ambulance, but it was too late; Bridgette had been pronounced dead on arrival.

"Is Mr. Kennedy gonna be okay?" Sloane asked for the fourth or fifth time.

"We think he is," Noah told her.

Gabby chimed in. "He's a healthy man. Healthier than a lot of younger people." It sounded like she was trying to convince herself as well as Sloane.

"Or he might die, like Mommy." Sloane said it in an oddly peppy way. Her eyes, though, were wide and hollow looking.

Noah's chest tightened. Sloane was remembering the same experience he'd been thinking of.

Noah met Gabby's eyes over his daughter's head as he leaned over and put a hand on her back, rubbing it. "No, honey. Mommy was in a terrible accident. Mr. Kennedy is just…sick."

Gabby stroked Sloane's hair, and Sloane leaned into her. Noah was grateful to have her there. Clearly, she was a comfort.

"Why was he acting so funny?" Sloane asked.

"We'll find out soon, I hope," Gabby said. "Maybe he took the wrong medicine, or has a fever. The doctors will figure out what's wrong and how to help. They're very smart."

Over the PA system, a calm voice announced, "Code Blue, fourth floor. Code Blue, fourth floor." There was a *beep-beep-beep* sound from outside, an emergency vehicle backing up.

"Your daughter is beautiful." The comment came from a middle-aged woman sitting across from them.

"Thank you," Noah said, and smiled. Gabby and Sloane smiled at the woman, too.

"You look just like your mommy, honey," the woman said. "I'd know you were mother and daughter any day."

Noah froze. On Sloane's other side, Gabby had gone still, too.

Sloane looked up at Gabby.

Another announcement over the PA system. "Mrs. Fletcher, please come to the reception desk. Mrs. Fletcher."

"That's me." The woman who'd made the "mommy" comment gathered her things and hurried away.

"I don't look like Mommy," Sloane said. "She's dead."

Noah drew in a breath and looked at Gabby.

She was looking back at him steadily.

"Why did that lady say that?" Sloane asked.

Noah held his breath. Was this the moment?

He was confused about everything. He was full of memories of Bridgette's death. Worried about Mr. Kennedy and how Sloane would react if he were seriously ill. Unsure about Gabby, whether she was exactly who she said she was.

He didn't know what to do.

Gabby lifted an eyebrow. Clearly, she was asking his permission to tell Sloane the truth now. Right now.

Back when things had been clearer, he and Gabby had made the plan of telling Sloane on Friday night.

It was Friday night.

Would there ever be a perfect time?

He met Gabby's eyes and saw the steadiness there, the care. He nodded once, giving her the go-ahead.

He saw her suck in a deep breath. "You look like your birth mommy, Sloane," she said.

Sloane frowned up at her. "Do you know her?"

Gabby glanced at Noah.

He leaned over and took Sloane's hand. "There's something we want to tell you." He smiled, kept his voice steady and reassuring, hid his own mixed opinions.

"Something good?" Sloane asked.

"Yes." He hoped so. Was pretty sure it was good. He sucked in a deep breath. "Honey, Miss Gabby is your birth mother," he said.

Sloane's eyes went impossibly wide. She looked up at Gabby.

"Yes, honey, it's me," Gabby said. She smiled at Sloane and put an arm around her.

Sloane twisted away and stared at Gabby for a long moment. Then she bent over her coloring book, gripped a crayon tightly, and scribbled black clouds into the sky.

This wasn't the way Noah would have chosen to do it, and it wasn't the way he'd have expected Sloane to react. But the truth had to be revealed sometime, and it was never going to be easy. "Do you want to talk about it, muffin?" he asked.

"Do you have any questions?" Gabby added.

Sloane stared down at the coloring book, her forehead wrinkling. Then she slid off the chair, took a couple steps away from both of them, and hurled the coloring book at Gabby, hitting her square in the chest. "Why didn't you keep me?" she yelled.

Chapter Thirteen

Gabby was still shaken two hours after the ill-advised reveal.

Sloane's tantrum had been monumental. It had rocked the hospital waiting room. She'd kicked and cried and tried to hit Gabby and Noah both. A security guard had actually come over to find out what was wrong.

Noah had finally picked her up and carried her outside, thrashing and screaming, while Gabby dealt with the details of Mr. Kennedy's release.

That part was the good news. Mr. Kennedy's dizziness and confusion had resulted from a simple case of dehydration. After receiving IV fluids, he'd emerged walking normally, waving away the hospital aide who'd been assigned to help him make his exit and apologizing for the trouble he'd caused.

Noah had driven them home, Gabby in the front seat, Mr. Kennedy and a crying, angry Sloane in the back. Once they'd reached the cottage resort, Gabby had helped Mr. Kennedy into the house and made sure he had plenty of food and drink available.

Noah had disappeared into his cottage with Sloane.

Gabby had texted Noah to see if she could help, or at least talk to Sloane.

Tomorrow, he'd texted back.

That left Gabby to replay the waiting room scene over and over in her mind. What had possessed her and Noah to let a stranger's comment dictate the revelation of such an important truth to Sloane?

The rage and pain on Sloane's face had gutted her. Gabby wasn't shocked that her daughter would be angry about the situation, but she'd been stunned by the immediacy and intensity of Sloane's emotions. It had been worse than the worst-case scenario in Gabby's mind.

She wanted to kick herself. As a second-grade teacher, she knew what kids were like. She should have anticipated that Sloane would react the way she had.

Sloane couldn't understand what had caused Gabby to make the incredibly difficult decision to place her for adoption. No seven-year-old could. And there was no opening to tell her, not now. Gabby was left with a heart full of sympathetic pain and personal guilt.

Now, she had to decide how to punt. What was the right next step?

She could go over there now, insist on talking it through with Sloane. But that wasn't her right. Noah was the real parent. He'd raised Sloane and knew her best. He'd said they needed to wait until tomorrow, and he was probably right.

Even then, though, what could Gabby say? Should she tell a seven-year-old that her birth father was a dangerous man? Or leave that out and take the entire blame for the adoption, making herself seem like she'd placed Sloane on a whim, or because she didn't want her?

It was an impossible situation. Gabby's heart broke for Sloane and the pain she must be feeling, but she was helpless to mitigate it.

She'd heard it said that being a parent meant wearing

your heart on the outside of your body. Your child's pain was your own. Now she was experiencing it: Sloane's hurt and rage about being cast aside were sharp knives cutting into her own heart.

Adoption was a wonderful way to build a family. But from the birth parent end of things, there was always going to be pain.

Gabby had managed to keep the pain locked inside her heart for the past seven years. She'd told herself Sloane was better off with another family and had tried to leave it at that.

Now, suddenly, she was deeply involved with Sloane and Noah, and the pain she'd buried had erupted. If she'd kept Sloane, could she have evaded Todd and raised her with all the love in her heart? Had she given up too quickly, been too cowed to do the right thing?

Poor Sloane. Her anger tonight had been a cover-up for sadness and grief, and there was no way for Gabby to help her with it, not now.

All she could do was go to bed, Caramel in her arms, and cry—and pray for wisdom. She had to figure out the best way to help a little girl deal with the pain of being abandoned.

Pain Gabby herself had caused.

Noah had hoped Saturday would be a restful day, but it wasn't starting out that way.

"I don't wanna help!" Sloane raised the small bag of groceries Noah had handed her and hurled it to the ground.

Yogurt, red raspberries and pears splattered out onto the driveway and splashed up onto Noah's pant legs and Sloane's shoes.

"My shoes!" Sloane danced around, stomping her feet, trying without success to get rid of the food stains on her new sneakers.

Noah sighed. It was 10:00 a.m., and he was already exhausted. He dug around in the remaining grocery bags, opened a container of paper towels, and handed a couple to Sloane. As he wiped off his own jeans, he surveyed the food-covered driveway. He'd hose it down later, after getting the rest of the groceries inside.

Sloane scrubbed at her shoes, then looked up at him with teary eyes. "They're still dirty," she said.

"We can hose them off when we wash down the driveway. They'll be fine. But we won't have fruit or yogurt for breakfast this week." It was a natural consequence, supposedly the best kind.

"But I want fruit and yogurt!" Sloane wailed.

Noah did, too. He'd been looking forward to enjoying that big container of succulent red raspberries, in particular. "Now, you can help me bring in the rest of the groceries without throwing anything or spilling anything. Or you can have a time-out on the steps while I do it."

She ran to the steps and sat, burying her face in her hands.

Noah carried in the rest of the groceries. The best way to help Sloane deal with the shocking revelation that Gabby was her birth mother, he'd decided, was to stick to their routine. They'd always done chores on Saturday morning, so they'd spent a little time straightening up the house and then gone to the grocery store. Sloane had done okay—not great, but okay—until they'd gotten home from the store.

He suspected the sight of Gabby's place had undone her.

He also suspected that Gabby had heard Sloane's screams, but she hadn't come out. That was probably best. The poor woman had to be exhausted and upset after Sloane's reaction to learning she was her birth mother.

Noah would get in touch with her later. For now, he had

to focus on Sloane: calming her down and helping her deal with the new knowledge she'd gained last night.

Quickly, he put away their groceries, setting aside the food they'd purchased for Mr. Kennedy. Then he went back outside, sat down on the steps beside Sloane, and put an arm around her. "Want to help me wash off the driveway and your shoes? And then we can go check on Mr. Kennedy, take him the things we bought for him."

"He would have liked the yogurt and raspberries." She looked up at him, tears standing in her eyes. "I'm sorry, Daddy."

"It's okay. We still have plenty of things to give him." He stroked her hair.

She leaned against him. "I wanna see Caramel."

That gave Noah hope. Caramel was a link to Gabby. "Maybe later, but first let's clean up and deliver our gifts to Mr. Kennedy."

"Okay."

She was subdued as they hosed off the driveway and her shoes, not even giggling when he directed a little water toward her now-bare feet.

Poor kiddo. Any kind of change was hard for her. A big mental shift, like finding out the identity of her birth mother, took more coping skills than she had at age seven. He should have seen that coming and managed the revelation of the truth more carefully. Throwing it at her casually in a hospital emergency room, already a fraught environment for both of them, had been an incredibly foolish move. Especially when she was already worried about her beloved Mr. Kennedy.

He sighed. It wasn't the first parenting mistake he'd made, and it wouldn't be the last.

Twenty minutes later, they were in Mr. Kennedy's house, sitting at his kitchen table. The older man was impeccably dressed, his color returned, and he insisted on serving them glasses of lemonade. Sloane watched Atticus run on his hamster wheel, and she explained to Noah that animals needed exercise every day, just like people. Mr. Kennedy nodded and smiled, clearly proud of his student.

"I sure do appreciate your help last night," Mr. Kennedy said, looking from Sloane to Noah. "I don't know what would have happened if this little lady hadn't seen that I was sick."

"I thought you were drunk, like Mommy used to get," Sloane said matter-of-factly.

Noah's face heated. He didn't like the fact that his child knew what an intoxicated person looked like, but there it was.

"Would you like to do a project for me?" Mr. Kennedy asked Sloane now.

"Yeah!" she said.

"All right." The older man led her onto his back porch. Noah watched from the kitchen table, amused, as Mr. Kennedy pulled out a big jar of change. Noah couldn't hear what Mr. Kennedy was saying to Sloane, but she was nodding, wide-eyed.

Together, they dumped the money out onto the floor, and then Mr. Kennedy set out four smaller jars. He showed her how to sort the coins into quarters, dimes, nickels and pennies, putting each type of coin in its own jar. Then he returned to the kitchen.

"Thank you," Noah said. "She loves to have a job, or at least, she loves to have a fun job like sorting money."

"All children do, I think." The older man sat down across the table from Noah. "I used to help my grandparents when I was about Sloane's age. Sorting my grandpa's nails and nuts and bolts, or my grandmother's buttons…lots of happy memories."

Noah hadn't known his own grandparents, and Sloane

barely knew hers. "You're a wonderful new friend for her," he said. "She was worried when she saw that you were sick."

"Thought I was drinking like her momma, huh?" Mr. Kennedy raised an eyebrow.

Noah spread his hands. "Unfortunately, that's what led to my late wife's car accident and death."

"Sad." They sat quietly for a moment, sipping lemonade, watching Sloane sort coins. "She's had a time of it, hasn't she? You both have."

Noah couldn't deny it. He just nodded and took another sip of lemonade.

"As far as drinking goes," Mr. Kennedy said in a brighter tone, "I wasn't drinking enough. Water, that is. I learned my lesson. Dehydration is a risk, especially for us older folks."

"I'm glad that's all it was, and that you're better," Noah said.

"I'm better," Mr. Kennedy said, "and Sloane seems better than she was last night, too. What was that all about?"

Since Mr. Kennedy had already heard the gist of it, mostly from Sloane's angry shrieks all the way home last night, Noah explained the situation. "This whole move was about getting her in contact with a solid mother figure, her birth mother," he said. "Now, I'm wondering if that was all a mistake. Wondering…" He trailed off.

"Go on." Mr. Kennedy stood and opened a window. A breeze blew the curtains, and the sound of a songbird and someone's lawn mower drifted in.

"I'm wondering if Gabby's a fit mother," Noah admitted. "Wondering if she placed Sloane for adoption for selfish reasons. Wondering if she's going to get back together with her ex and run off, out of Sloane's life."

Mr. Kennedy put his hands on his hips. "I'm surprised you'd say that, even just knowing Gabby for a few weeks.

The woman loves kids. She wouldn't have given up a child unless there was no alternative. Of that, I'm absolutely sure."

Noah blew out a sigh. "I wish I could be that certain."

"Stick around awhile, get to know her better. You'll see." He came back to the table, propped his hands on the edge of it, and leaned toward Noah. "Seems to me your late wife may have more to do with your attitude than any actual facts about Gabby."

Noah frowned. Was that true?

"Read your Bible," Mr. Kennedy advised. "I once made a study of all the verses about the past. Mostly, they were about leaving the past behind. None of them said to dwell on it."

"I don't think I do that, exactly." Noah leaned back and crossed his arms. "Too busy with the present. With her." He gestured toward Sloane.

Mr. Kennedy straightened. "Forgetting those things which are behind, and reaching forth unto those things which are before, I press on toward the mark for the prize of the high calling of God in Christ Jesus." He smiled. "That's from Philippians, chapter three, verses thirteen and fourteen. You may think you're not dwelling in the past, but are you pressing forward, looking toward Christ?"

"I don't know—"

"Old things are passed away; behold, all things are become new!"

"Corinthians?" Noah guessed.

"Second Corinthians, chapter five, verse seventeen. I could go on, but I think you catch my—or rather, God's—meaning."

Some people might find Mr. Kennedy's lectures annoying or pedantic. Not Noah. He looked with respect at the older man. "How'd you memorize all that? Do you have a verse for every occasion?"

"Pretty much." Mr. Kennedy sat down again. "In my day, in my small town, that was Sunday school. I'm still proud of the prizes I won for it. But more than that, it's served me well in life. If you can call to mind a verse that fits what's troubling you, you can figure out what to do."

"Good point." Noah had been quick to judge Gabby, especially after seeing that photo of her with her ex. What no one else knew was that his wife had cheated on him with two different Washington, D.C. go-getters. He'd tried to tell himself that it was her alcoholism that had caused her to stray, but deep inside, he'd felt hurt and insecure because of her behavior. Maybe that was why he'd reacted so strongly to seeing that photo at Gabby's place. Maybe it had more to do with his own history than with anything in her personality.

Maybe he needed to forget what was behind, let it pass away. Let the past be the past. Reach toward the future and toward Christ.

Mr. Kennedy was right: the Gabby he was coming to know was a good person, unselfish and caring. She wouldn't have given Sloane up for selfish reasons, no way. And she wouldn't lie to him about her ex being dangerously abusive. Nor would she go back to an abuser; she was too strong for that.

His heart felt lighter suddenly, as if a weight had been lifted.

The increasing responsibility he'd felt for Sloane as Bridgette had proven she wasn't up to motherhood had pressed down on him for those few years. That was something he'd known before. What he hadn't realized was that it had misshaped him, making him a suspicious, untrusting person who dwelled too much on past history. Making him less effective as a father, and certainly not anyone's idea of a good life partner.

He wanted to go back to the man he'd been before all the heartbreak and difficulty. Wanted to be the man who was excited about writing books for readers to get lost in, over-joyed to be a father, eager for the next adventure. Wanted to be a man who could love a good woman.

He was still thinking about that as he admired Sloane's coin-sorting success and bid Mr. Kennedy goodbye.

They walked back toward their own place, and Sloane held his hand and looked up at him. "Can I see Caramel?" she asked.

"Well…that's up to Miss Gabby."

"My…my…"

"Your birth mother," he said quietly.

"My birth mother." She repeated the words carefully, as if she were learning a new language.

He squeezed her hand. "Let's fix our lunch, and I'll text Miss Gabby and see what she has planned for today," he said. "Maybe we could do a short visit with her and Caramel."

"Okay!" Sloane jumped a little, and hope rose in Noah's chest. Was it possible that this was going to be easier than it had seemed?

He looked toward Gabby's cottage and his steps slowed.

There was a man at her door, knocking, then ringing the doorbell. A man who looked a little bit familiar.

When the man turned as if to walk away, Noah realized why he seemed familiar. It was the man from the photo he'd seen. Gabby's ex.

The man returned to the door and spoke, then opened the screen and walked inside.

Noah's heart started pounding, too hard, too fast. "Race you to the cottage," he said to Sloane, making his voice ex-cited.

She laughed, a happy sound, and took off toward their

house. Noah followed more slowly, letting her win while he took a quick glance back toward Gabby's place.

There was no sign of either her or her ex. Her door was closed.

So much for reaching toward the future. It looked like Gabby was turning away from him and Sloane and back toward the past.

How was he supposed to feel now? What was he supposed to do?

Gabby's heart pounded double-time as she looked at the man she'd once loved. It was, in a way, her worst nightmare: he was here, in her cottage. She was alone with him.

Only being alone with Todd wasn't her worst nightmare, not anymore.

When she'd opened the door and seen Todd there, she'd wanted to slam the door in his face. But over his shoulder, she'd seen Noah and Sloane walking across the grass, headed toward their cottage.

Anything was better than having him see Sloane and becoming suspicious. If that woman in the waiting room had noticed the resemblance, then Todd, as observant as he was, could notice, too.

"You're looking good, Gab," he said, opening his arms and moving toward her.

She took a giant step back. His words and attempt at a hug sent a brief memory through her, a memory of the time when he'd been her world, when she'd loved him more than she'd loved herself.

Now she just wanted to let him know she wasn't interested. She wanted to send him packing before he saw Sloane and put two and two together. "We're divorced," she said to him. "I don't want to talk to you. What are you doing here?"

From her perch on an ottoman, Caramel barked.

"Oh, but you let me in, didn't you?" he said, his handsome smile going a little crooked. "You always did put up a little resistance. Didn't quite know what you wanted."

She straightened her spine. "I know what I want," she said. "I want you out of my life. No letters. No visits. Go back to wherever you're living now. We're through."

His face flushed red, and a vein stood out in his forehead. He uttered an awful name he'd called her many times before.

Shame washed over Gabby, slick and sickening. What a dolt she was. Misguided, wrong, bad. Only a fool would let herself get trapped in a small cottage with this dangerous, evil man again.

The old insecurity and self-hatred rose inside her. She was worthless, just as Todd had said.

She drew a deep breath, glanced over at Caramel, and saw a photograph of her and Aunt Dee, coming in from a boating trip, happy and smiling.

Aunt Dee had counseled her with such wisdom when she'd come to live in Chesapeake Corners, when she was still raw and devastated by her marriage and by having to place Sloane for adoption.

Sloane. This horrible man had taken Sloane from her. Gabby wasn't the bad person. Todd was.

Righteous anger swept her shame and fear away.

She was a child of God. She was strong, stronger than she'd ever realized.

She'd done the hardest thing a woman could do—give away her child, for the child's greater good—and she'd survived it. Now, somehow, God had brought good out of that horrible situation. He'd brought Sloane a wonderful father, and He'd brought her back to Gabby.

She had a chance to be a real mother now, to the daughter

she'd never stopped loving since placing her for adoption. "Go on now," she told Todd, gesturing toward the door. "Get out and don't come back. I have absolutely no interest, and if you bother me again, I'll get the police involved."

"You wouldn't dare," he sneered.

Caramel jumped down from the ottoman and walked toward Todd, barking.

Gabby looked back to the photo of herself with Aunt Dee, and inspiration struck. She slid her phone out of her pocket. "I'm videoing you now," she told him, holding it up and bringing him into the camera frame. "And I have good neighbors who'll come if I scream, which I *will* if you take one step closer."

He narrowed his eyes, and she swallowed hard. Just around the eyes, when he was angry, she could see the way Sloane looked in her worst rages.

"Go on," she said steadily. "Get out of my home. Now."

He cursed, turned, and walked to the door, nudging Caramel out of the way roughly with his foot. The little dog yelped and ran behind a chair.

Gabby's jaw clenched.

"I'll be back for you," he warned, "and you'll come with me. Or you'll pay."

"Threat recorded," she said into the phone, adding the date and time.

He called her another ugly name and stormed out of the house.

She locked the door behind him, trembling with delayed terror. She watched until he drove away, thinking at the last minute to photograph his car, though it was probably a rental and it was too far away to get the license plate, anyway.

You did it, she told herself. *You got rid of him.*

Around the edges of her fear, a little bit of pride glowed.

She'd stood up to Todd, to his face. She hadn't let him intimidate her nor talk her into letting him back into her life.

And yes, she'd enraged him. But she didn't have to be driven by fear of his rage, not anymore. When faced with having his actions recorded, when he'd realized she wasn't afraid—or at least, that she wasn't giving in to her fear—he'd backed down.

She had to be cautious, still. She absolutely had to protect Sloane, which probably meant letting Noah know Todd had come around, and her aunt, too, and even Mr. Kennedy.

She had to be safe, but she'd seen her ex-husband's weaker side. She'd stood up to him. She was stronger.

She was never going to let him control or ruin her life, never, ever again.

Chapter Fourteen

The day after seeing Gabby's ex go into her home, Noah tried to push the sight, and his jealous thoughts, out of his mind.

He had had one goal in attending Dee's Fall Party: he was going to enjoy this beautiful autumn day with his daughter.

He was *not* going to worry about Gabby.

Dee had called and asked him to take Mr. Kennedy's place at the grill, so that the older man could take things a little bit easy. Noah was glad of the job.

He'd learned to act like an extrovert at times, both in his military career and while doing public appearances as an author. But the truth was, he'd rather be one-on-one than at a crowded party any day of the week.

Manning the grill would give him something to do so that he didn't have to spend every minute socializing.

The fact that Gabby would be there filled him with a complex mix of feelings. Maybe, busy with grilling, he'd just ignore her. He knew what Mr. Kennedy had said was true: she was a good person who wouldn't have placed Sloane for adoption without a good reason. That reason, she'd told Noah, had been her ex.

But then she'd let her ex into her house yesterday. Why?

And there he was, doing what he'd vowed not to do: worrying about Gabby.

He and Sloane heard the party before they rounded the corner and saw the large crowd gathered in the cottage resort's common area. He'd been told that the Fall Party was for long-term residents, celebrating the end of tourist season and the resumption of everyday life. Noah had imagined that only the ten or twelve year-round residents would attend. But apparently, people from the surrounding neighborhoods had been invited, too; he recognized some of them from walks he'd taken in the area.

"There's Penelope!" Sloane gave a little leap. "Can I go play with her, Daddy?"

"Of course you can." He watched her run to the other little girl. Friendship and active play would do a lot for Sloane's mood, which had been up and down today. Kiddo was getting used to the idea of a birth mother, but the adjustment would take time.

Gratitude rose in him, gratitude for this little community that had welcomed Sloane in, for the friends who'd accepted both of them despite their flaws and weaknesses.

He approached the grill, and Aunt Dee came bustling over, a tray of burgers and crab cakes in her hands. "I'm glad you're here, and if you don't mind, I'll put you to work right away. People came hungry."

"No problem." He knelt to figure out how to light the grill.

"Gabby!" Dee called. "Can you come help with this?"

Noah's heart skipped a beat.

"Sure," came that easy, friendly voice Noah liked so well.

From his crouched position, he saw Gabby's sandals and bright pink toenails, the fun side of her always peeking through.

But he also noticed the way her steps slackened when

she got closer. Close enough to see him, no doubt. Slowly, he stood.

"Oh, hey!" She gave him a tentative smile. Well, why wouldn't she be tentative with him? When she'd texted asking how Sloane was doing, his responses had been terse and noncommittal. He'd put off the idea of getting Gabby and Sloane together.

Dee gave Gabby a quick side hug. "Do you mind helping Noah with the grilling? It's really a two-person job. Someone needs to run around getting sauces and plates and more of everything to cook, while the other person grills."

"And gets all the glory," Gabby said wryly. "I'm familiar. Glad to be the gofer, since I'm not a pro at the grill."

"Perfect. I'll leave you to it." Dee hurried off to greet some new arrivals.

"Did she do this on purpose?" Noah wondered aloud as he took plastic wrap off a plate of burgers. "And also, I'm going to need some seasoning salt and another pair of tongs."

"Probably. I'll go get stuff." She swept back into the house.

As she returned, friends kept stopping her, greeting her, talking to her. At first, he thought she must have something going on, some news, but then he realized she was just friendly and popular. She tucked her hair behind her ears and laughed with a couple of women, and then helped a child find her mother. He noticed several men watching her, and why not? She was lovely.

The question was, was she going back with her ex?

Noah knew he needed to put the past behind him. He'd looked up the Bible verses Mr. Kennedy had quoted, and done an internet search for more. He'd even written several of them out on index cards and was trying to memorize them.

It helped. But he knew that in order to put the past behind him, he had to accept what had happened and deal with it.

His ex had cheated on him, and it had not only infuriated him, it had dealt his self-confidence a blow.

Now, seeing a group of dads gesture for Gabby to come over, telling her something that made her laugh, he doubted his own appeal.

He was an introvert and tended to brood. What would someone like Gabby see in a man like Noah?

Why was he thinking that way? The whole point of getting over his past was so that he could deal with Gabby in a calm way, work with her, cooperate with her. Gabby was the birth mother of his adopted child, and a teacher in Sloane's school. That was all there was to his relationship with her. Wasn't it?

She returned to the grill with the supplies he'd requested, and for a while they were both busy, cooking food and taking it out to the long serving tables. They worked together well, communicating with glances and quick words.

When their duties slowed down briefly, she leaned against a chair and looked up at him. "How's Sloane doing?"

"Up and down," he said truthfully. He flipped a couple of veggie burgers.

"I thought you'd be in touch about getting together with her," she said. "Don't you think that would be wise, rather than letting her stew about me being her birth mother without spending any time with me?"

"Yeah, well… I don't know." He turned down the grill. *Don't hide what you're feeling. Deal with it.*

He lifted his chin and looked at her. "I saw your ex come to your door yesterday." Even saying the words aloud made him angry and insecure.

"You saw him?" Her voice rose to a squeak.

He nodded, waiting.

"I didn't want to bring it up and ruin the party, but that was terrifying," she said. "He was all smiles at first, but pretty quickly he reverted to his old self. Yelling at me, threatening me. It was awful."

Instantly, his jealousy fell away and was replaced with a sense of shame. Gabby had been in trouble, and he hadn't helped her. He'd stayed away, jealous, thinking something romantic was going on.

He'd been a jerk.

His jaw clenched. He hated the thought of anyone yelling at Gabby, threatening her. "Why didn't you call me? I would have come to help."

"Exactly what I wanted to avoid," she said. "I wouldn't have let him in at all, only I saw you and Sloane outside and I didn't want him to see her and realize our connection."

He had to agree that she'd done the right thing. "Did he hurt you in any way?" If he had, Noah would hunt the man down.

To his surprise, she chuckled. "I started recording him and I threatened to call the cops. He was angry, but when I didn't back off, he left." Her expression sobered. "I'm definitely concerned that he'll come back. We should all be on our guard."

"Does he know about me and Sloane living next door? Does he know Sloane's your child?" She was Todd's child, too, only the man was no father.

"I don't think so." She waved to a couple of people arriving at the party. "He didn't mention it, and he would have if he knew. But still…"

"We need to be cautious and aware."

"Yes. I'm hoping that I scared him away with my video and threat to call the police. He's never seen my strength before, not really."

"I hope so, too." Noah's tight shoulders relaxed a little. The ex was a threat, but not in the way Noah had thought.

Gabby didn't want to be with him. She'd stood up to him and was proud of it.

They dealt with another flurry of requests—more burgers, more brats—and Noah found himself enjoying their teamwork. Gabby was a good grill partner, not complaining about having to run back and forth, anticipating his needs before he realized them himself sometimes.

During another lull, he asked her whether she had any ideas about next steps with Sloane. "We didn't choose the best time to tell her the truth, but it would have been upsetting to her anytime. She's thinking it through, and I think she'll come around to see that it's a good thing." He smiled, and added, "She keeps asking to play with Caramel. I think that may be code for she wants to see you."

"Caramel first, I'm sure." Gabby smiled. "I know my place in the priorities of a seven-year-old. But you know what? I have an idea. Can you handle the grill alone for a few?"

"Of course." He watched her head toward her cottage.

It was strange. Two hours ago, he'd been focused on his anger and insecurity about Gabby. But after spending time with her, working and talking together, everything had changed.

Just being with her made him feel less alone. Just as they'd been good partners at the grill, maybe they could be good partners in parenting Sloane.

What she'd said about her ex was concerning, but he also felt lighter and happier after hearing her side of it. She wasn't yearning for the guy; she was working to keep him away and keep Sloane safe.

That was what he needed to focus on, too: keeping the guy away. He had trouble seeing her ex as a risk, maybe because the guy was significantly smaller than Noah and didn't look really athletic. He had that thin, stylish look that was popular nowadays.

It was also good news that he'd caved and left at the threat of police. Still, if Gabby saw him as dangerous, Noah needed to believe her and take precautions.

Which reminded him—he hadn't seen Sloane in a while. He flagged down Dee. "Have you seen Sloane and Penelope?"

"Hmm." She looked around. "They were playing on the swings for a while, and I saw them with a couple of other kids. Want me to take over while you track them down?"

"Yes, please." Concern tugged at his stomach. She was probably fine, and yet…he wanted his eyes on her, especially after the conversation he'd just had with Gabby.

He strode around the party and didn't see the kids. Or wait. A group of them came running around the cottage.

Sloane wasn't there.

Gabby approached him from the direction of her cottage, Caramel on a leash and a picture book in her hand. "What's up? You look worried."

"I can't find Sloane."

She tilted her head to one side. "Where was she last?"

"She was with Penelope." A slight chill ran down Noah's spine. "They were playing on the swings."

Could her ex have figured out Sloane's relationship to him and to Gabby? Could he have lured her away?

Gabby lifted her chin. "We'll find her. Let's ask some of the other kids."

"Good idea." He was grateful she was here. He needed her help.

They had to find Sloane.

Gabby marched over to the group on the playground, Noah

following behind as she scanned the area. "Do you know where Sloane and Penelope are?" she asked the kids.

A couple of the boys shrugged, but the third boy pointed toward the bay. "I think they went that way."

Noah's heart rate accelerated. "Let's go," he said to Gabby, adrenaline making him move quickly.

"Wait," Gabby said.

Noah turned back, impatient.

She knelt in front of the child who'd pointed them toward the bay. "Do you remember what they wanted to do down by the bay? Did you actually see them go?"

He shrugged and loped off toward his friends.

"We don't have time to waste," he said. "I'm headed down there."

She touched his arm. "I know that kid. He tends to make things up. Let's not go off half-cocked."

He gulped down breaths to keep from yelling at her. "What do you suggest?" he managed to say as he scanned the party, looking for his daughter. What had she even been wearing today? Why couldn't he remember?

Why hadn't he kept a closer eye on her?

The groups of people talking, the music, the kids' game of tag and the adults' cornhole tournament all made it hard to look.

If her birth father had gotten to her…

Gabby touched his arm again, this time leaving her hand there. "Wait. I think… Is that Penelope?"

"Daddy!" The sound of Sloane's happy, excited voice made his tight shoulders relax. He let out a relieved breath as Sloane and Penelope ran toward them. He knelt down, and Sloane crashed into him, hugging him.

He held onto her until she struggled. "Where were you?" he asked.

"This one guy has a giant turtle," Penelope said.

"It's a *tortoise*," Sloane corrected. "He said we could come see it."

"So we did go." Penelope was holding a rubber ball, and she tossed it into the air as she spoke. "Then we remembered we're supposed to stay where you can see us, and we came back." The two of them beamed, obviously proud of their good behavior and oblivious to the anxiety they'd caused him and Gabby.

He stepped closer to Gabby. She must have had the same impulse, because she moved closer, too, until their arms were almost touching. They faced Sloane and Penelope, shoulder to shoulder.

"You gave us a scare, girls," Gabby said. "Are you allowed to go off with a stranger?"

"He's not a stranger," Penelope said. "He's my mom's brother's boss. Or…my mom's brother is *his* boss. Something like that."

The corners of Gabby's mouth twitched. "Small town," she said to Noah.

"Penelope? There you are." Penelope's mom marched over. "I've been looking for you. Where have you been?"

"Looking at Uncle Bob's boss's turtle," she said.

"Tortoise," corrected Sloane.

"Oh. Well, you know better. You're not allowed to run off like that. Come on, we're leaving."

"No!" Penelope said.

"No!" Sloane echoed.

The girls acted like it was the tragedy of the century, hugging each other and promising to walk to school together the next day.

"Whew," Gabby said when they were alone, just the three

of them. "I'm so glad you're here and safe and sound." She patted Sloane's shoulder, hesitantly.

Sloane looked at her searchingly but didn't speak.

Around them, people were getting ready to leave, snapping photos of themselves and their friends and families with Aunt Dee's pumpkin decorations.

Gabby knelt in front of Sloane. "I heard you might want to see Caramel," she said. "And I have a new book that I think you might like. Want to read to her?"

Noah winced. He wasn't sure putting on the reading pressure was the right thing to do at this point, when Sloane had so much to get used to.

But Sloane nodded. "Okay, Miss Gabby," she said, and the two of them walked over to where someone was holding Caramel. Moments later, Sloane was sitting on a bench, Caramel beside her as the little girl appeared to read. True to her usual teaching technique, Gabby had backed off to give child and dog space.

He came over and stood beside Gabby, both of them far enough behind the reading pair to be out of earshot. "I'm surprised that worked, but I'm glad."

She nodded. "It occurred to me that she might be more comfortable with my teacher side, for now," she said. "Anything that builds our relationship."

"You're smart, you know that?"

"Thanks for noticing!" She gave him a saucy grin. Their eyes met and held. Then she turned away, still smiling. "I can bring her home, if you want," she said.

"That sounds good." He actually welcomed a little time alone to ponder the day.

He'd wanted to have a calm and relaxing time for him and Sloane, and to get her used to the idea of having a mother—

a different mother. And it looked like that part was happening, but the day had been anything but relaxing.

He looked skyward. He and Sloane had gone to church that morning, and the sermon had reminded him that he needed to put his cares in God's hands. Of course, he knew that, but as a fallible human, it seemed like he needed to be reminded over and over again. So as he walked, he prayed. *Father, please help Sloane and Gabby build a good connection. Bless them both.*

He went on home and sat on his porch and enjoyed the breeze, trying not to think too hard. He was getting the feeling that things might just work out.

After Noah left, Sloane complained that it was too hot sitting on the sunny bench. So Gabby, Sloane and Caramel retreated to the front porch of Aunt Dee's cottage to finish their reading activity.

Sloane perched on one end of Dee's old-fashioned glider, Caramel cuddled next to her and the book Gabby had chosen in front of her.

Gabby sat on the other end, not pushing to join in the cuddle session, but ready to stay close if Sloane was open to it. Especially given the book she'd chosen. She wasn't sure if it was perfect, or way too close to home.

"If you want," she said, "I can read it to you, and then you can read it to Caramel." Sometimes, a struggling reader did better if they knew the general storyline before reading a story themselves.

"I want to read it to Caramel," Sloane said. She looked down at the Yorkie, whose black button eyes watched her with apparent curiosity.

Sloane opened the book and smiled to see a picture of a

little girl and a dog. "My mom luh…luh…" She broke off and looked at Gabby.

Gabby made a heart shape with her hands.

"My mom loves…me," Sloane read.

Gabby inhaled a stuttery breath. This was the right thing to do. Books were always a good way to help kids understand difficult topics. She believed that with her whole heart, and had recommended books to parents helping their kids deal with divorce or loss or change.

Now that she was the parent, though, it felt different. Risky. Terrifying. Would this story help Sloane, or alienate her?

Sloane was having no such worries, apparently. Her eyes squinted and her forehead wrinkled as she sounded out words. Slowly, she worked her way through the story about a puppy whose mother couldn't take care of her. The little dog was fostered by another dog family, but the birth mother trotted over and checked on her whenever she could. Then the puppy was adopted by a human family. Emphasis in the story was on the love for the little dog, love of all parties.

Sloane was interested enough to work hard at reading the book, and Gabby, watching her, felt tears push at the backs of her eyes. She was helping her daughter read a story. Helping her daughter understand *their* story.

Caramel rested her head on Sloane's leg, looking up at the little girl as if she were listening.

When Sloane closed the book, Gabby clapped softly. "You read the whole book! That's great!"

Sloane smiled. "I did it!" She patted her lap, and Caramel climbed in and licked her face.

"Way to go, honey," Gabby said. "You're being so gentle with Caramel, too." She knew it might take time for Sloane to process the story and think about how it applied to her own situation. She also knew that kids needed repetition.

Just being here, sitting here with her daughter, talking with her and praising her ability to learn and be gentle…it was enough to make Gabby's heart full.

Sloane petted Caramel for a few minutes, then looked around the now-empty yard. She hadn't looked at Gabby yet, or at least, she wasn't focusing on her.

That was okay. But before child and dog got restless, she decided to end the session. Less was more. It would be better if Sloane ended their reading time wishing it could go on longer, rather than longing for it to end.

Probably better if time with her birth mother stayed brief, too. It was so much for Sloane to process. Gabby was happy things had gone as well as they had.

"Time to go home," she said, standing. "It'll be fun to tell your dad how well you did, won't it?"

Sloane nodded and climbed off the couch. Then she looked up at Gabby. "Did you check on me after you gave me to Mommy and Daddy, like in the story?"

It took a moment for Gabby to understand what Sloane meant. Then she blinked. It sounded like Sloane had not only processed the story, but she'd compared it to her own situation and was asking questions. "It's not so easy to do that with kids as with puppies," she said. "Your adoption was a closed adoption. Did your mom and dad ever talk to you about that?"

Sloane shook her head. "They said my birth mother couldn't take care of me."

"That's right. At that time, I couldn't. But I was allowed to talk to the social worker who helped with the adoption. She let me know how you were doing." Gabby reached out and touched Sloane's shoulder. "I loved you and thought about you every single day."

"Why couldn't you take care of me?" Sloane pressed.

Gabby had thought she was prepared for the question, but she hadn't anticipated what it would be like to answer it with her daughter's intent eyes on her. "Your birth father was…is…not a nice man," she said. "He's, well, he's sick. He has a mental illness that makes him rough. Too rough for a child to be around."

"Oh." Sloane scratched Caramel's ears.

"To keep you safe, I had to let the social worker find you another mommy and daddy." Gabby's eyes filled with tears. "But I never ever stopped loving you."

Sloane eased out from under Caramel and stood. "Okay. I have to go home now."

"Caramel and I will walk with you," Gabby said. They walked the half block to their cottages.

"Are you sad?" Sloane asked.

Gabby nodded. "I am."

"It'll be okay, Miss Gabby." Sloane took her hand, and they walked together.

Chapter Fifteen

After all the excitement of the weekend, Noah was glad he and Sloane could have a quiet week. She went to school and behaved fairly well there, aside from a minor yelling match with another kid that earned her a day without recess. As for Noah, he'd written hard every minute she was gone, and his first draft was over half-done. The regular schedule calmed them both down.

Sloane had read with Caramel one afternoon, and they'd seen Gabby briefly while working in the yard. But she'd been busy with school, and she'd texted him that she was keeping it low-key, giving Sloane the chance to get used to all that was new.

It was a smart decision, but Noah missed seeing her.

On Friday afternoon, satisfied with his accomplishments for the week, Noah found himself at loose ends. Sloane was having a sleepover at Penelope's house. He'd thought of asking Gabby to get together or hang out…he'd been thinking of it all week, in fact. When he'd encountered her at the mailboxes, though—and yes, he'd timed his mail collecting trip to coincide with hers—she'd said she was meeting Angie for dinner.

So that meant he had solitude, something he normally enjoyed. But as it got later in the afternoon, as a light rain started to fall, he realized his brain was stuck in a revolving door of thoughts and feelings. Most of them were about Gabby and Sloane.

Noah had come to Chesapeake Corners on a fool's errand, to try to connect with Sloane's birth mother to help Sloane heal. With the help of God, and Aunt Dee, he'd achieved that goal.

As it turned out, Gabby was so much more than he'd expected. His own feelings for her were stronger than he'd ever felt for a woman. Gabby could fit so perfectly into his small family, and every male instinct told him to push it further.

His fatherly, protective side argued against that. He'd trusted his wife to stay the course, to keep the same goals and plans as they'd started out with. But she'd steadily changed into someone he didn't understand. Someone who wasn't a good mother, wasn't interested in being one.

Fool me once, shame on you. Fool me twice, shame on me.

Finally, he put on a rain jacket and walked down to Dee's cottage, in search of a way to get out of himself. She was sitting on her covered porch and quickly beckoned him in, out of the rain.

"Anything I can do for you?" he asked her. "I've got a free evening, and I'm handy with small repairs, if the cottages need anything."

"You're a good man." Dee stood. "And if you're open to doing me a different favor, you're an answer to prayer. I need to pick up some custom cabinets in Baltimore, and I've been dreading the drive. Rush hour traffic, and I don't like driving at night. Feel like being my chauffeur?"

"Of course, I'm glad to drive you." He smiled. "As long as you don't mind talking about something with me, helping me think it through."

"I have the feeling I know what that something is. So maybe we're an answer to one another's prayers."

The drive up the shore was just what Noah needed. Sun peeked out between rapidly moving clouds, casting a silvery light over the marshes and fields. Fishing boats bobbed in the bay. Dee was knowledgeable about the area and had answers for most of his questions. She was basically a research gold mine for someone new to the area and writing about it.

They talked and laughed the whole way to the carpentry shop, and he loaded the cabinets into the back of his SUV.

They drove home as the sun sank behind them, slipping between colorful clouds and casting a golden light. Traffic was brisk, and they made good time.

"So tell me how it's going with Sloane and Gabby," she said.

"Really well, I think." He steered around a slow-moving sedan. "They've talked one-on-one a few times, and Sloane threw out 'my birth mom' when she was talking to Penelope's mother today."

"Wow, she's accepting it easily," Dee said, and then held up a hand. "Mind, if she's anything like the fosters I've raised, she'll cycle back to upset and grieving periodically through the years."

"It's Sloane," he said. He knew his kid. "I don't expect her to be steady and docile for long. Still, I'm pleased."

"Yes! It's going well. We did well."

Traffic slowed down as they approached the Chesapeake Bay Bridge. "It's seven thirty," Noah said. "A little late for Friday night rush hour, isn't it?"

"Not here," she said. "Everyone drives out from the city to the Eastern Shore on Friday nights."

That made sense. "I'm in no hurry," Noah said. "I don't have anywhere else to be."

An old compact car put on a signal in front of them, and he slowed to let the car in. "I guess we did do well," he said, picking up the conversation where they'd left off. "You helped me find Gabby, and it looks like she'll be a good strong mother figure for Sloane. She'll fill up the gap my late wife left in her life."

They were both quiet for a minute. Then Dee chuckled. "I'm sensing there's a little more you need to work out."

"Yeah." He glanced over at her. "It's Gabby. I like her a lot."

She smiled. "I could tell. You like her as more than just Sloane's mom. Right?"

Was he that obvious? He sighed. "I'd like to date her, to be honest. But what if it doesn't go well? Or what if it *does* go well, and then later on she changes her personality? I feel like I can't take that type of risk when Sloane's emotional health has been so precarious."

Even as he said it, he realized he was doing what Mr. Kennedy had told him not to do. What his Bible had told him not to do. He was living in the past.

Apparently, foster kids weren't the only ones who needed to cycle through their history again and again before healing was complete.

"Your wife changed on you," Dee said.

"Yeah," he said. "It turned out motherhood was just a passing whim."

Dee blew out a sigh and patted his arm. "That's awful." After a minute, she spoke again. "Gabby's not like that. She's consistent. She was the kind of kid who kept going to the special buddies club when all the other students moved on to other things. Didn't want to disappoint the kiddos in the club."

Noah nodded. He could see Gabby doing that. She was kind and liked helping people.

"And when I had some health problems and needed help with the cottages, she came to help with no questions asked. That was five, almost six years ago, and she's been an incredible gift to me."

"You're a gift to her as well. I can see that."

"She's my family. I don't have anyone else, aside from a few distant cousins." She straightened her shoulders. "The only thing missing from my life is a little one to love, and maybe that won't be missing for long."

"Maybe not." When he'd come here, he'd thought primarily about the benefit to Sloane. Now, he realized that the change would affect others, too. Gabby, of course, whose life would change at the foundations. But also Dee, who sometimes let a little wistful loneliness slip out past her active, peppy persona.

"The point is," Dee said, "if she commits to Sloane, it'll be for keeps. I suspect your real worry is that she might leave *you*."

He glanced over at her. "What?"

"Didn't your wife change in her attitude toward you, too? Not just toward motherhood?"

"She did," Noah said slowly.

"Well, Gabby's a different person. If she commits to you, she won't flip-flop on it later. But—" She held up one finger. "If you do get close with her, be good to her. She was badly hurt by that jerk of an ex."

"So I hear," Noah said. They'd come through the tollbooth, the last barrier before the bridge. "The good news is, she said she'd overcome her fear of him. She realized it when he visited."

"What?" Dee sat up straight and leaned forward, eyes on his face. "Todd visited her? Here? Lately?"

"Oops." Noah winced. "I thought she would have told you."

"No, because she knew I'd freak out. That man threatened her life, Noah."

A faint uneasiness crept up Noah's spine. He hadn't realized it was that serious. Gabby hadn't specified what he'd done to her, and Noah had assumed he'd pushed her around physically, which was bad enough. "He wanted to kill her?"

"Came at her twice," Dee said. "Once with a knife and once with a gun. She was able to talk him down both times, but he wasn't kidding."

"That makes me admire what she did even more, when he came to her place last week," he said as they crested the arch of the bridge. "She videoed him, and let him know neighbors were within earshot, and told him she'd call the police. He took off."

"Hmm." Dee sounded skeptical. "Do you know if he left the area?"

"When I asked her a couple days ago, she hadn't seen him again."

"Well, that's good." Dee turned in her seat to look behind them. "I should be enjoying God's glorious sunset, not borrowing trouble."

Noah glanced in the rearview mirror. Behind the line of cars, the setting sun burned red and orange, sending flickers of fire out into the darkening sky.

Dee was right. It was glorious, and whatever his personal worries, he was grateful for the beauty around him.

His phone pinged with a text. "Want me to look at it?" Dee asked.

"Please."

"It's from Penelope's mom."

Noah's heart rate jumped a few levels. He told Dee his passcode.

She read the text. We think Penelope broke her arm. Headed to hospital. Dropping Sloane off.

"Call her," Noah said. "Put it on speaker. Please."

Penelope's mom picked up. "Hey, Noah," she said over the sound of Penelope's crying. "Just pulling up to your place."

"I'm not there," Noah said.

"Hmm. Gabby's place is dark. How about I leave her with Dee?"

"I'm here with Noah," Dee said. "We're about an hour away."

"I can stay with Mr. Kennedy," Sloane piped up.

"Is that okay? We're keen to get Penelope medical attention. Not a serious break, we hope, but she's hurting."

"Well, sure," Noah said. "If he says it's okay. If not, take her to the hospital and we'll swing by when we get back to town." Mr. Kennedy wasn't the strongest physically, especially since he'd gotten sick. But he was so smart. If something went wrong, he'd know what to do.

"Will do." Penelope's mom ended the call.

Traffic slowed to a crawl again, and a light rain began to fall.

"Sorry I got you into this," she said. "I didn't realize traffic would be this bad."

"I drove in DC for years," he said. "I'm used to traffic." The truth was, he'd enjoyed the challenge of DC driving, navigating crowded highways at high speed.

Another text pinged into Noah's phone, and Dee read it off. "She's with Mr. Kennedy. He was happy to help."

"Good." Noah felt his shoulders relax. Sloane would be fine there. Although the older man could be crotchety, Noah was learning that he had a warm heart underneath. And Sloane loved him.

Dee looked at her phone. "Mrs. Rennicker took a nice picture of you and Sloane and Gabby at the party."

Since they'd ground to a halt—must be an accident up ahead—he looked over. Sloane sat on a bench, reading to Caramel. Gabby and Noah stood together in the background, looking on from a distance, both smiling.

His heart warmed as he remembered the moment. He wanted there to be more pictures like that. He was starting to think he wanted Gabby in their lives, for real and for keeps.

"Do you mind that she tagged your author page?" Dee asked.

An ambulance and a police car were making their way along the berm, confirming Noah's guess that an accident was causing the delay. It took him a minute to process what Dee had said. "Wait," he said, frowning. "That picture is on social media?"

"Uh-huh."

"That anyone can see."

"Ye-esss," Dee said. "Oh, no. I'll get her to take it down."

Noah gripped the steering wheel tighter. Why would anyone post a picture of a child publicly? He'd never understood that, though plenty of people did it.

In Sloane's case, though, there was one big reason not to post her image: Gabby's ex-husband, Todd. "I don't like it," he said, craning his neck to see how close they were to breaking free of the traffic jam. Not close at all, unfortunately.

"Nor do I." Dee was sitting upright now, peering worriedly out the windows. "Although, what are the odds that he'd happen to see it?"

Her phone pinged and she looked down, then scrolled. "She took the photo down," she said. "Apologized for posting it. But…she said it's been up a few hours."

Noah focused on driving as traffic started to move, although way too slowly for Noah's taste. He wanted to get to Gabby, see for himself that she was okay, that her ex hadn't seen the photo and come after her. And although he knew Sloane was safe with Mr. Kennedy, he wanted to see her, too.

Gabby and Angie sat in Angie's car, windows open slightly to let in the cool air. A light rain was falling. They were in Gabby's driveway, but neither was quite ready for the evening to end.

They'd had a delicious taco dinner and lots of conversation about therapy dogs and about adoption, since Angie and her husband, Luke, were planning to adopt. Only on the drive home had Gabby gotten the chance to tell Angie about the progress she'd made in connecting to Sloane.

Now Angie asked, "Can you adopt her back somehow?"

Gabby smiled and shook her head. "That's not how it works. But Noah wants me involved in her life. And Sloane is coming around."

"Of course she is," Angie said. "You're a wonderful person. And whether you're legally her mother or not, you'll be a great mother figure to her."

"That's all I want."

Angie nudged her. "Is it, though?"

"What do you mean?"

"I mean, I've seen the way you and Noah look at each other. Maybe you could be a mother to Sloane by joining her and Noah's family another way."

Gabby's face burned. "Oh, well... I don't know. He's a great guy, for sure. And a wonderful father."

"And he looks at you like you're a queen," Angie said. "Which is how he *should* look at you. You deserve to be treated well, Gab. You deserve all the happiness in the world."

Gabby reached over and gave her friend a one-armed hug. "Thank you. You're a sweetheart."

Outside the car, the rain intensified. "I'd better get inside, and you'd better get home," Gabby said. She got out of the car as her phone buzzed. She rushed to get under the awning, then waved Angie away. "I'm fine," she called. "Go on home before it gets too bad out." Caramel was barking inside, and she opened the screen door and looked down at her phone.

Angie tooted her horn and drove away.

The text was from an unknown number.

I saw you with our daughter.

Gabby gasped. There was only one person who could have sent that message.

She fumbled for her key and opened the door.

Suddenly, a hand grabbed her phone and then shoved her inside.

Caramel, barking frantically, ran out into the rain.

And Gabby struggled out of Todd's grip and turned to face him.

Chapter Sixteen

The traffic had lightened up considerably. Noah and Dee would have made good time were it not for the sheets of rain, slowing everyone down and hindering visibility. "Will you call Mr. Kennedy?" Noah asked. He was hunched forward, trying to see the road. "Tell him it'll be a little longer than we expected."

"Sure thing." Dee called from her own phone and put it on speaker as she explained the situation to Mr. Kennedy.

"That's just fine." Mr. Kennedy's voice was faint. "We're having ourselves a ball here." There was some muttering. "Now, how do I get this thing on speaker?"

He heard Sloane's voice. "Right here. Tap that." And then her voice became louder. "Guess what, Daddy! Guess who just came over?"

Relief flowed through Noah at the happy, unworried sound of his daughter's voice. "Miss Gabby?"

"No. Caramel!"

Noah glanced over at Dee, who looked puzzled. "Caramel's there but Gabby isn't? Did she drop her off?"

"No! Caramel came over by herself!"

Mr. Kennedy took up the story. "We heard her barking. You know how loud she is, for such a little pup. We just brought her in. Soaked like a drowned rat and running all around."

"She looks so funny, Daddy!"

Noah's stomach tightened. He swerved to avoid a fallen tree branch.

"We're thinking about taking her back, but it's raining cats and dogs here."

Sloane chortled. "You're silly, Mr. Kennedy. It can't rain cats and dogs!"

"I want you three to stay put," Dee said. "We'll be there in half an hour."

It was an optimistic estimate, but one Noah intended to make true if possible.

Dee ended the call. "I don't like this," she said. "Gabby wouldn't have let Caramel out alone, especially in a rainstorm like this. I'm going to try her again." She placed the call, but there was no answer.

Sloane was miles away with a frail elderly man and a Yorkie. And Gabby wasn't answering her phone.

Noah stepped on the gas.

Gabby stood behind an armchair, her heart pounding, her hands shaking. Todd was in the middle of the room, ranting, calling her awful names.

"You betrayed me," he said, his voice low and furious. "You're with someone else. Someone who looks at you like you're a queen." His voice rose to a mocking treble on the last words.

He'd overheard her and Angie talking. Gabby's stomach lurched. If Todd thought she was with someone else, she was in trouble.

Swallowing hard, Gabby forced herself to think. All the

murder mysteries she had read portrayed cool detectives getting the villain to talk.

But Todd didn't need any prompting for that.

Thunder boomed outside, and Gabby cringed, thinking of her tiny dog out in the storm. Caramel wasn't one of those dogs who hid under the bed every time she heard thunder, but she did get nervous. And that was when she was inside a warm, dry house with Gabby. How must she feel, running alone in the rain?

Gabby stepped to the side of the chair that was closest to the door. "Just hold on a minute," she said. "I have to get my dog. She'll be scared in the dark and the rain."

"Little rat dog," Todd said, his lip curling. "Forget about her. I want to talk about that guy you're with now. Who is he?"

Did he mean Noah? Who else could he mean? "My life isn't your business, Todd. We're divorced. Let me get my dog."

"I'll tell you who you're with," he snarled. "It's some famous writer."

How did he know that? She took a step toward the door.

Todd sidestepped, blocking her. "How do you have our child? I thought you lost her."

Gabby blew out a breath and tried to keep her face from showing the sudden terror she felt inside. How did Todd know she was their child, and that Gabby had connected with her?

At least Sloane wasn't home. In the struggle with Todd, Gabby had seen that Noah's house was dark. Noah must have taken Sloane somewhere, but what if they came back?

Noah was strong and courageous and an experienced military cop.

But Todd was dangerous, even more unhinged now than he'd been when he and Gabby were married.

She prayed silently, desperately. *Lord, keep Sloane safe. And Noah. And Caramel.*

Todd took two giant steps and grabbed her by the shoulders, pulling her into the middle of the room. "Tell me!" he yelled, shaking her with every word. "Where is our child?"

All the years she'd been away from Todd, all the strength and courage she'd gained, fell away, and she was that young wife again, terrified of what her husband would do to her, fearful that if she even tried to stop him things would get much, much worse. Sweat dripped down her back and her heart thudded painfully.

She closed her eyes. And then a voice inside her spoke, almost audibly.

No way he's doing this to me again. No way.

She straightened her spine. She wasn't weak and terrified, not anymore. She wasn't giving in to Todd's cruelty and aggression. If she had to go down, she'd go down fighting. Maybe it had taken her a few minutes to remember that she wasn't the same person now, that she was stronger. Years of abuse never entirely left you.

But she'd grown and she'd changed and she had a child to protect. And a dog. And a man she'd come to care about, who had no idea this monster was here, right next door to his home.

She stomped down hard on Todd's instep. "Let go of me."

"Ow!" He winced, and his face reddened. "You little..." A stream of curses came from his mouth and he gripped her shoulders harder.

He might be mad, but Gabby was furious. Because of him, her dog was out in the rain. Because of him, her child was at risk.

She glanced out the window. Good. Noah's cottage was still dark.

A sudden longing rose in her. She wanted Noah here. Wanted to be able to lean on him. Didn't want to do it all alone.

But he *wasn't* here. This situation was on her. She twisted and shoved, and maybe it was because he wasn't expecting it, but Todd's hands came off her shoulders.

"I'm going out to find my dog," she said, stepping toward the door. "You'd better be gone when I get back."

He grabbed her arm, squeezing it so hard that she couldn't help crying out. "You're not going anywhere." He took a handful of her hair and yanked it.

Pain shot through her, and with it, a flashback to the helpless fear she'd felt before, when Todd had gotten violent. Worse was to come, she knew that.

And she wasn't letting it happen. She elbowed him hard, and then spun toward him and kneed him harder.

He screamed and doubled over, his hands dropping away from her to hold his stomach.

Lightning flashed, and she glanced out the window.

A sudden coldness hit her core.

Mr. Kennedy was coming toward her cottage, holding a giant umbrella over Sloane, who had—was that Caramel in her arms?

She had to keep them away, keep them safe. She flicked a lamp on, hoping it would allow them to see her. After making sure Todd was still doubled over, she gestured them away with both hands, like a traffic cop.

She couldn't tell if they saw, but she had to hope so. Todd was straightening up now, and she looked around, frantic. How did you knock someone out? Her self-defense class had been all about getting away from an attacker, but right now, she didn't want to get away, not if doing so would lead Todd to Sloane. She needed to incapacitate him.

Her large, annotated Bible was on the table beside her

chair. "I'm sorry, God," she whispered. She picked up the book and brought it down on Todd's head, hard.

He went down on one knee, but didn't fall to the ground unconscious, as she'd hoped.

The lights flickered, then went out. She could only pray Mr. Kennedy and Sloane weren't about to come barging in.

"You're going to pay," Todd snarled. He struggled to his feet and came at her.

Chapter Seventeen

Noah pulled into his driveway. Through the pouring rain, his headlights caught two figures on his front porch, one tall and stooped, one small.

He cut the engine, rushed through the rain and swept Sloane into his arms, relieved beyond measure to find her safe.

Mr. Kennedy was talking rapidly to Dee, but Sloane's excited voice covered whatever he was saying. "Daddy! Caramel came to get us!"

He caught the word *Gabby* in Mr. Kennedy's conversation and put Sloane down, keeping a hand on her shoulder. "Where is she?"

"She's in her place," Mr. Kennedy said, gesturing toward Gabby's cottage. "We think she's in danger but she waved us away."

Caramel yipped and struggled in the older man's arms.

"Call 911," Noah said.

"Already did. Police are coming as fast as they can."

"I'll stay here," Dee said. "You go help Gabby."

"Want my .38 Special?" Mr. Kennedy asked.

"No guns," Dee said. "We'll pray. Let's get Sloane inside." She led Mr. Kennedy, Sloane and Caramel into Noah's cottage.

Noah decided against taking the time to get his own

weapon, locked away for safety. He ran across the yard, shoes sloshing, getting soaked to the skin.

He peered in through the small window beside the front door. Any noise he was making was covered up by the driving rain. With no lights, it took him a few seconds to see through the dimness and understand what was going on.

Gabby was pinned against the wall. A man he recognized as her ex had her by the shoulders and was yelling into her face.

Rage made the edges of his vision red, hyperfocusing him on the scene inside. Gabby was speaking, not yelling back, her face in a forced-relaxed expression.

The man drew back a fist.

Noah burst through the door.

He grasped the man's shoulders and yanked him off Gabby. He held out a hand to make sure she didn't fall, then threw the man to the ground face down. A knee on his back held him there, though unfortunately, it didn't close his foul mouth.

How had Noah ever thought the man would be attractive to Gabby? Noah looked up at her. "Did he hurt you?"

"I'm okay." She crooked her arm to hold one hand close to her chest, then touched an abrasion on her cheek. "Glad to see you, though."

The jerk had hurt her, and Noah put more of his weight onto the man, whose curses changed to whimpers.

Sirens sounded, distant and then coming closer.

"I'll direct them," Gabby said, her voice a little hoarse. She limped across the room.

It took everything Noah had to stop himself from beating the miserable excuse for a man now whining on the floor.

The door opened and two officers entered, and after making sure they had control, Noah stepped away. Within a minute they had Todd in handcuffs.

Noah followed the police outside as they half carried and half dragged Todd, then threw him into the cruiser.

Gabby stood on the porch to one side, holding Sloane against her, keeping her face turned away from the man. Mr. Kennedy and Dee flanked them, one on either side. Caramel was in Dee's arms.

Sloane tried to twist away from Gabby, but Gabby knelt and put a hand on either side of Sloane's face. "Don't look," she said. "Don't you look."

It hit Noah hard: the jerk in the back of the cruiser was Sloane's biological father. And Gabby didn't want the image of him in handcuffs burned into Sloane's brain.

She was protective to the core.

He moved toward them, knelt, and wrapped his arms around the two of them, his heart rate slowing a little. They were safe.

One of the officers emerged from the cruiser. "We're going to need to talk with you, ma'am," she said. "You too, sir, but that can wait until tomorrow."

Gabby looked up at Noah. "Keep her—keep them—safe."

He squeezed Gabby's hand. "I will," he promised. "And we'll keep Caramel at our place until you're done."

He took Sloane inside and listened to Mr. Kennedy's excited explanations and Dee's questions. He held onto Sloane and Caramel, both of them getting sleepy. And he counted his blessings and thanked God for His protection.

After a few minutes, the elders went to their respective cottages to change into dry clothes, promising that they'd be around to talk tomorrow.

At that point, Noah realized that he, Sloane and Caramel were all still soaked. He toweled off the little dog and helped Sloane change into warm pajamas. Then he eased her into bed, giving in to her plea that Caramel be allowed to sleep with her just this once.

It was Caramel who'd alerted Mr. Kennedy and Sloane to Gabby's trouble. The little dog had run around the house barking, unwilling to settle down and relax. The behavior had been unusual enough that Mr. Kennedy had decided to call the police.

Noah scratched the Yorkie's ears and promised her a gourmet meal tomorrow.

Then he watched over girl and dog as they drifted off to sleep.

They were safe. Gabby was safe. He took deep, thankful breaths.

It had been a close call. He should have taken the risks more seriously. Should have watched out for photographs that could eventually be posted for the world to see. Shouldn't have gotten caught up in jealousy about Gabby's horrible ex.

He'd known—mostly—that Gabby was telling the truth when she had explained that she'd chosen adoption because her ex was a bad and dangerous man. Now, he'd seen it with his own eyes.

His feeling when he'd seen her at risk had been akin to what he'd feel if someone were hurting Sloane: primal protective rage that someone was harming his family.

He wanted to see Gabby, talk to her. But after all that had happened, how would she react to him?

Fear that he hadn't responded well enough, that he'd pushed her away, sent a panicky feeling through him.

He couldn't let her slip away.

As he watched Sloane sleep, and listened to Caramel's delicate snores, he made a plan.

Gabby spent Saturday recovering from Friday night.

Aunt Dee insisted on taking Gabby to an urgent care facility, where she got her sprained wrist wrapped and her broken toe taped. She paid a brief visit to Mr. Kennedy and to Sloane and Noah, making sure everyone was okay and reassuring Sloane that they were all safe.

Later, she'd figure out with Noah, and maybe a family therapist, how to explain to Sloane that her birth father was the one who'd attacked Gabby. For now, though, it seemed good to let Sloane focus on the exciting adventure they'd had and the role she'd played along with Caramel and Mr. Kennedy.

Todd was in custody and the legal process would work itself out. Gabby wasn't looking forward to testifying, but she was no longer intimidated by her ex-husband. She'd seen, last night, how truly small and powerless he was. Yes, he'd hurt her physically, but with her newfound strength and with her supportive friends around her, she'd made it through his attack relatively unscathed. If he ended up with a short sentence or, God forbid, going free, she'd deal with it when the time came. And thinking of Caramel, Aunt Dee and her cottage resort family, she knew she wouldn't ever have to face him alone again.

On Sunday, they were almost back to normal, except they all seemed to want to be together. They went to church together, Aunt Dee, Mr. Kennedy, Noah, Sloane and Gabby. Afterward, Mr. Kennedy suggested a boat ride, and they spent the sunny afternoon on the bay.

Gabby loved watching Mr. Kennedy and Sloane together. The man was still cranky at times, sensitive to noise, precise about routines and rules. But he also laughed at Sloane's and Caramel's antics. When Sloane cuddled up close beside him, his eyes got a little shiny. He was a wonderful stand-in grandfather for Sloane.

Apparently, Dee was seeing new sides of him, too. She kept looking at him with appreciation.

As the boat docked at the end of the afternoon, they grabbed pizza together and then Dee offered to take Sloane home. Mr. Kennedy quickly offered to walk along with them.

Gabby glanced at Noah. He was smiling at Dee and Mr. Kennedy, and she saw him mouth, *Thank you*. What was he planning?

"Want to take a stroll along the bay?" Noah asked. "We can keep it short. I don't want to strain your foot."

"Sure," she said.

They walked a little, with Gabby holding Noah's arm for support, and then stopped at a bench looking out over the water. The air was cooler, and the sun was setting sooner these days. It sank into the bay, and the sky glowed purple and orange and gold.

Noah took her hand, and she looked over at him.

He was smiling at her. She squeezed his hand, and he lifted hers and kissed it.

His gentle touch brought home that no, all men were not alike. Something she'd known in her head but not her heart. Noah wasn't an abuser like Todd had been. He would never hurt her. Instead, he was a protector.

But was there more? He'd kissed her hand. Did he feel something special for her?

"Do you—"

"I realized some things—" he said at the same time.

"You first," Gabby said.

Noah cleared his throat. "You know," he said, "I was influenced by my ex, too. She wasn't there emotionally, and she cheated. Worst of all, she neglected Sloane. It affected me more than I realized."

"I get that." And she did. She herself had been impacted by her past in ways she hadn't realized until recently.

"I've been hesitant to get into a relationship because I worried that other women would be like her. I worried about getting you involved with Sloane because I didn't quite trust that you'd be reliable."

"Of course. You had to be careful."

"Yes, but there's such a thing as being too careful. Now that you're in her life, Sloane is much calmer and more resourceful. Trusting you was the right thing to do."

"I'm glad," she said. His words were a balm for her heart, which still sometimes struggled with guilt for letting Sloane be adopted.

"I'm wondering if…well, if you'd be interested in taking things further."

"Meaning…" Gabby's heart pounded.

"Dating," he said. "I'd really like to date you."

Gabby sucked in a breath. Fear and excitement warred in her, along with a little insecurity. "Is this because Sloane needs a mom?"

He smiled a little and shook his head. "She does, and you're a wonderful one. You will be, regardless of how you respond. But the main thing is, Gabby… I'm in love with you."

Her stomach dropped. Had he said…

"You're courageous and resourceful and beautiful," he said. "I don't want to be away from you. I want Sloane and me to stay in Chesapeake Corners, and I'd like to give this thing between us a try. I know it's new, we haven't known each other long and there's so much to process, but can you at least think about it?"

She looked out to the bay, her heart leaping. A shorebird flew low over the water, then dove in, coming up a minute later with a fish.

She'd wanted a child and she had Sloane now. The legalities were to be decided, whether she could possibly even adopt Sloane back.

Noah was watching her, his brow furrowed.

Did she want a relationship with Noah? Could she get past her old fears and try again?

For just a moment, she thought of Todd's hot breath on her face, his harsh words in her ears, his hands on her body, hurting her.

But that was Todd. Noah was an entirely different man. Strong and loving and sure. A rock she could lean on.

Heat radiated through her. She caught her breath and looked into his eyes, and certainty washed through her. "I do want to try it. I do want to be with you."

He touched her face, his expression still a little insecure. And she didn't want him to feel unsure, not after all he'd been through. She had to say more, spell it out. "When I saw you come in on Friday night, it was such a relief. I needed you. But also, I was terrified he'd do something to you and I would lose you."

"No chance of that," he said with masculine confidence. He put an arm around her. "I felt the same, when I saw him pinning you to that wall." He looked over at her. "Well, not the same. I was furious. I wanted to hurt him."

"You seemed pretty mad," she said, remembering how he'd pulled Todd away from her, as if her scary ex were just a child. She leaned away so she could look into his face, his eyes. "I care about you, Noah. I love your creativity and the way you parent Sloane. You're strong and protective and… well, I think you might just be what I want."

A breeze lifted a strand of her hair, and before she could brush it away, Noah did. He let his hand stay there, gently tangled in her hair.

She drew in a breath and let it out slowly, and looked into his eyes. She couldn't yet say *I love you*. It was too soon. But she could say what she felt. "I do want to try being with you, Noah. I can't *wait* to try it."

He pulled her close and held her, and Gabby knew she was exactly where she belonged.

Epilogue

On a crisp, late fall Saturday, Gabby sat on her steps, her heart contented and full.

Noah was in the side yard raking leaves. Mr. Kennedy strolled with Aunt Dee, both of them talking with animation.

Sloane lay on her side on a plaid blanket, reading to Caramel.

All the changes the child had been through still triggered her ODD occasionally, and she was seeing a family therapist along with Noah and sometimes Gabby. The therapist had helped them explain Todd to Sloane. They'd found an age-appropriate way to let her know that he was serving time in prison, since it turned out that Gabby wasn't the only woman he'd assaulted. It was all terribly sad. The therapy was focused on Sloane, of course, but it was helping Gabby to heal, too.

She watched Sloane read, her finger guiding her along the lines, sounding out words. She was doing well with reading now and liked it, for two reasons. One, of course, was Caramel. The other was that Noah had written, and was writing still, an ongoing children's story geared to Sloane's reading level. It was all about Princess Sloane and her mother, Queen Gabby.

In a way, his skill at this writing project was more impressive to Gabby than his successful adult thrillers. He kept the story going, with new episodes every few days. He got Sloane to illustrate the story. And he'd learned all about writing for kids with reading issues, using a select vocabulary along with high-interest content. Gabby wouldn't be surprised if he ended up publishing that type of book as a sideline.

Aunt Dee and Mr. Kennedy had stopped to chat with Noah, and now they came over to where Gabby was sitting. "You should go listen to this part of the story," they said. "Noah thinks you'll find it interesting."

So she walked over and cuddled up on the blanket with Sloane. "Keep reading," she said. "I just came to listen."

Feeling the warmth of her daughter in her arms, watching Caramel's alert button eyes and glancing over to catch Noah's smile, Gabby felt truly blessed.

"Look at the new pal," Sloane read carefully. "It is Sir No… No… Noahhhh." She wiggled in Gabby's arms. "Like Daddy!"

"Good job sounding it out!"

Sloane read on. "'Come with me,' the new pal said to Queen Gabby. 'We will take a walk.'"

She turned the page and frowned, puzzled. "That's the end of this part."

Caramel yipped.

Gabby was pleased with Sloane's reaction. It meant she was learning the structure of a story, which would help her reading comprehension.

Hearing a sound behind her, Gabby looked up. There was Noah, holding out a hand. "*Will* you walk with me, Queen Gabby?" he asked.

"Of course, fine sir!" Gabby rose, smiling. She and Noah had gotten so close in the past couple of months. She loved seeing his funny, playful side. They'd taken many wonderful long walks together, sometimes with Sloane, sometimes alone. She never got tired of talking with him.

Sloane was giggling. "He's Sir Noah!" she said to Aunt Dee as the older woman walked toward them.

"Indeed he is," Aunt Dee said. "Would you come help me with a chore, Sloane?"

Sloane stood slowly. "Okay," she said. "What chore? Can Caramel come?"

"Baking chocolate chip cookies. And yes, Caramel can come."

"I'll help!" Sloane took Aunt Dee's hand, and the two of them walked off toward the woman's cottage, Sloane holding Caramel's leash, without a backward glance. Their connection was growing by the day, and Dee talked often about how happy she was that Sloane had come into her life.

Gabby and Noah watched her go, then smiled at each other. It was wonderful being Sloane's parents together. It was more than Gabby had ever dreamed of.

They strolled down through town toward the bay. At first, they chatted about the day and the latest news, but as they reached the boardwalk, Gabby realized that Noah had gotten unusually quiet. "Is anything wrong?" she asked him.

"Not wrong. Right." He gestured for her to sit down on their favorite bench and then knelt in front of her.

Gabby's mouth went dry. Her heart pounded, faster and faster.

Noah kissed her hand. "You've made me so happy these past few months. I can't believe it, but I keep falling more and more in love with you."

She looked into his warm brown eyes. "I love you, too." She could say it now and mean it. Her doubts and inhibitions had flown away in the face of his goodness, of how right this felt.

"I can't wait to get started on the rest of our lives," he said, "and so, even though it's soon…" He trailed off and pulled a ring box out of his pocket. He held it up toward her. "Gabby, will you marry me?"

Gabby sucked in a breath. They'd talked about marriage, and she'd guessed from his getting down on one knee, but still...the force of this hit her like a tidal wave.

He was asking her to marry him. To spend their lives together. To make a family with him and Sloane.

The fishermen out on the dock, the swooping waterbirds, the rhythmic sound of waves lapping against the rocks below them...all of it faded away until the only thing she saw was Noah's dear face. "I want to be with you full-time, too."

"Is that...yes?" He tilted his head to one side. "You haven't even seen the ring."

"Yes!" She tugged at his hands until he rose to sit on the bench beside her. He pulled her into his lap, holding her as if she were made of precious and fragile glass. She leaned her head against his broad chest. "The ring's not important, compared to you," she said, "but...can I see?"

He opened the box. Inside was a band that looked like twisted vines, with a round diamond growing from them, like a flower.

Her jaw dropped. She looked up at him. "This is gorgeous! How did you know exactly the right one to get?"

Satisfaction crossed his face as he slipped it onto her finger. "I had a little help from Dee," he admitted. "You like it, then?"

"I love it. And you." She leaned into him, and he held her.

And Gabby realized that the past was truly behind her, and her future shone bright as the diamond she now wore. She closed her eyes and breathed a wordless prayer of thanks.

* * * * *

*If you liked this story from Lee Tobin McClain,
check out her previous Love Inspired books:*

Holding Onto Secrets
His Christmas Salvation
A Companion for His Son

*Available now from Love Inspired!
Find more great reads at www.LoveInspired.com.*

Dear Reader,

I hope you enjoyed getting to know Gabby, Noah, Sloane and, of course, Caramel the Yorkie.

This story holds a special place in my heart. I'm an adoptive mom, and I believe, just as Gabby says, that adoption is a beautiful way to form a family. At the same time, there is loss involved in any adoption. Birth parents, often out of love, have given their child to someone else to raise. And adopted children grow up to realize that their own story is more complicated than that of their friends.

I sometimes wonder about my daughter's birth mother, where she is and how she's dealt with the decision she made. Her circumstances were undoubtedly complicated, so complicated that I, and my daughter, will likely never get to meet her. *Her Surprise Neighbor* is my effort to imagine what adoption might feel like from her side.

Of course, being a romance writer, I gave Gabby, Noah and Sloane a happy ending! I hope their story lifted your spirits and warmed your heart.

Happy reading,
Lee

P.S. If you liked Angie, Gabby's friend and confidante, you can read her story in *Holding Onto Secrets*, recently released from Love Inspired books.